He set the photograph down to reach for the envelope again. When he pulled out the watch, Rafe's eyes widened and he let out a vicious curse.

He grasped the watch in one hand and yanked his cell phone out of his jeans pocket with the other.

"What's wrong?" Darby hated the alarm in her voice, but what had seemed like a harmless prank a few minutes ago now seemed like something far more sinister.

Rafe issued rapid-fire instructions into the phone. In answer to Darby's earlier question, he held the watch down where she could see it.

A stark digital readout flashed against the white background, displaying 00:00:15. The last number was decreasing—fourteen...thirteen...twelve. Rafe wasn't holding a watch. He was holding a timer.

And it was counting down.

He ended the call and looked at the timer. His gaze shot to hers. "Time's up."

Boom.

LENA DIAZ

EXPLOSIVE ATTRACTION

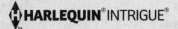

As always, my heartfelt appreciation goes to my editor, Allison Lyons, and my
agent, Nalini Akolekar. I am having a blast, and you are both to blame. To my
fellow Fire-Breathing Flamingos—Sheila Athens, Valerie Bowman, Alyssa Day,
Madeline Martin and Ava Milone—thank you for your awesome critiques,
your incredible brainstorming sessions and all those late nights at the Hen.
This book is dedicated to George, my incredibly patient and supportive husband
of more than twenty-six years. You taught me the real meaning of unconditional
love, and gave me the best gifts a woman could ever receive—our son, Sean,
and our daughter, Jennifer. I love you more than you will ever know.
I'm enjoying every chapter of this story
we're living together, and can't wait to see
what happens next.

ISBN-13: 978-0-373-74743-6

EXPLOSIVE ATTRACTION

Copyright © 2013 by Lena Diaz

Recycling programs
for this product may
not exist in your area.

HARLEQUIN®

™ www.Harlequin.com

Printed in U.S.A.

ABOUT THE AUTHOR

Lena Diaz was born in Kentucky and has also lived in California, Louisiana and Florida, where she now resides with her husband and two children. Before becoming a romance suspense author, she was a computer programmer. A former Romance Writers of America Golden Heart® finalist, she has won a prestigious Daphne du Maurier award for excellence in mystery and suspense. She loves to watch action movies, garden and hike in the beautiful Tennessee Smoky Mountains. To get the latest news about Lena, please visit her website, www.lenadiaz.com.

Books by Lena Diaz

HARLEQUIN INTRIGUE
1405—THE MARSHAL'S WITNESS
1422—EXPLOSIVE ATTRACTION

CAST OF CHARACTERS

Rafe Morgan—One of the best detectives on the St. Augustine police force, Rafe is also a trained bomb technician. After losing his wife in a brutal home invasion, Rafe is more determined than ever to make the streets of his hometown safe, and keep criminals where they belong—in prison.

Darby Steele—She became a psychologist to overcome her past and help others do the same. Her expert testimony often puts her and Detective Morgan on opposite sides in court. But after she becomes a serial bomber's obsession, she must turn to Rafe for help.

Jake Young—This St. Augustine detective and bomb-squad technician used to be Rafe's brother-in-law and his best friend. Jake can't get over his sister's death and Rafe's failure to protect her. But is he angry enough to turn to murder?

Captain Buresh—He oversees the serial-bomber investigation and may end up on the victim list.

Robert Ellington—The way this reporter covered Detective Morgan's wife's death made the two of them bitter enemies. How far will Ellington go for revenge and a story?

Nick Morgan—Brother of Rafe Morgan, Nick is a drug enforcement agent who helps Rafe and Darby when they are on the run.

Victor Grant—He is an assistant district attorney, and his death could be an important clue to the serial bomber's identity.

Judge Thompson—He presided over many of Rafe and Darby's court cases.

Clive McHenry—This private investigator knew Rafe's deepest secret.

Chapter One

The door to Darby's office flew open and banged against the wall. She froze in her chair, blinking in surprise at the man standing there, his dark eyes narrowed, intent, like a predator on the hunt.

Darby very much feared she was his prey.

"Where's the letter?" He stalked across the room, his laserlike gaze settling on her.

Trapped, between the desk and the wall. She pressed back against her chair while she mentally cataloged the office supplies around her for their weapon potential. She was reaching for her stapler when it dawned on her what he'd said, something about a *letter.*

Her young assistant stood in the doorway wringing her hands, glancing from the stranger to Darby. "I'm sorry, Dr. Steele. He refused to wait. He just—"

"The letter," the man repeated, his deep voice gruff with impatience.

That familiar voice had Darby letting go of the

stapler and studying him more carefully. Several days' growth of stubble darkened his jaw. His shaggy, unkempt hair hung just past his ears. His brows were a fierce slash on a deeply tanned face that would have been handsome if he wasn't frowning.

She'd been the recipient of that frown too many times *not* to recognize it.

Some of the tension drained out of her. "It's okay, Mindy," she reassured her assistant. "This is Detective Rafe Morgan."

A look of relief flashed across Mindy's face. Without waiting to see if Darby needed anything, she eagerly fled the office.

So much for having her boss's back.

Darby squelched her own desire to flee. Having Rafe Morgan burst into her office was only slightly better than confronting the drug-crazed stranger she'd first believed him to be. Especially since Rafe could barely stand to be in the same room with her.

The feeling was mutual.

Giving him the bland smile she reserved for her most difficult clients, she pushed back from her desk to shake his hand. "Detective, I almost didn't recognize you."

When he made no move to take her hand, she let out a deep sigh and dropped her hand to her side. Actually, the slight probably wasn't intentional. He seemed preoccupied, studying every detail in her office, as if he expected someone to jump out from behind a bookshelf or from behind the couch and chairs she used for her therapy sessions.

"You called the police, said someone sent you a threatening letter," he reminded her.

He was on duty, seriously? She glanced at the wrinkled shirt he was wearing and the equally wrinkled blazer that did little to conceal the large gun holstered at his waist. Since when had he started wearing jeans to work? Every time she'd ever seen him he was wearing a suit and tie, clean-shaven, with his dark hair cut military short. Then again, she'd only seen him at the courthouse, when they were both testifying—usually on opposite sides of a case. Maybe this was how he dressed when not in court.

He pulled a pair of latex gloves out of his jeans pocket and tugged them on. His gaze flicked down her suit, slowly, insultingly, past her skirt, down her legs to her heels then back up, before his mocking gaze met hers again.

Point taken. He'd noticed her looking at his clothes and was giving it right back to her. She wouldn't have expected anything less from him.

"I'm in a hurry here, Dr. Steele."

Her fists clenched at her side. "Of course. I wouldn't want to keep you here any longer than necessary."

The corner of his mouth quirked up. "Of course."

She gritted her teeth and whirled around, marching toward the grouping of furniture on the far side of the room. She reminded herself Rafe had lost his wife a year ago in a horrible tragedy. He deserved her patience and understanding. She drew a deep, bracing breath and stopped beside the couch. "I'm sure the letter isn't anything serious. I get things like this every once in a while."

"If you didn't think it was serious, why did you call the police?"

Patience, patience.

He stopped next to her, and she had to crane her neck back to look at him. In her calmest voice, she explained, "I have clients to think about. I never ignore threats, even if I don't think there's any real danger."

He seemed to consider that for a moment. "You get a lot of threats?" No sarcasm, just what sounded like genuine concern.

Darby let out a pent-up breath and moved past him to the small, decorative table where she kept her mail. "Two or three a year. People pin their hopes and dreams on a therapist. When things don't work out, they naturally blame me. Understandable." She reached for the large, padded manila envelope sitting on top.

Rafe grabbed her wrist in an iron hold.

She glanced up in question.

"The perp's fingerprints might still be on the envelope," he said.

"My prints are already on the envelope because I opened it. There's some kind of watch inside, and a piece of paper. I didn't pull either of them out, though, because as soon as I opened the envelope and saw what was printed on the paper, I put it down and called the police." She expected he'd praise her for her quick thinking in preserving the evidence, but he didn't say anything.

Instead, he picked up the envelope and peered inside. His entire body went rigid. "You saw the word *boom* written on the paper inside and didn't mention it when you called the police?"

She stiffened at his incredulous tone. "It's obvious there's nothing dangerous in there. I didn't want to raise alarms over a watch and a piece of paper."

He shook his head as if in disbelief. "Lucky for you, I'm a bomb tech and can verify the envelope does *not* contain a bomb. But *you* shouldn't have made that assumption. You should have reported exactly what you found and let the police handle it. If it had been a bomb, the person who responded to your call could have been killed if they weren't wearing a bomb suit or using the proper equipment."

Meaning *he* could have been killed. And of course, that *she* could have been killed when she'd first opened the envelope. Or even Mindy—

a single parent with three small children—when she'd brought the mail in.

That thought had Darby swallowing hard against her suddenly tight throat. "You're right. I'm so sorry. I didn't think about it that way. I would never purposely put anyone in danger."

His eyes widened at her apology. "No harm done," he said, sounding as if the admission had been wrung from him.

She frowned, thinking about his earlier statement. "Why would the police send a bomb technician without me mentioning the word *boom?*" She cocked her head to the side. "For that matter, when did you stop being a detective?"

"They sent *me* because I was the closest *detective* when your call came in. The bomb-tech part of my job is part-time, as needed." He reached into the envelope for the piece of paper.

"Makes sense, I suppose." She watched him pull the paper out and hold it up toward the light. "Actually, in a city as small as St. Augustine, I wouldn't expect we'd have a bomb squad at all. Doesn't the St. Johns County sheriff's office handle things like that?"

"We're perfectly capable of handling most suspicious-package reports without their help," he said, his tone sharp. "We just don't have the money for all the fancy equipment they have."

Sensing she'd stumbled onto a sensitive topic,

she nodded and watched him examine the paper. But when he flipped it over, she quickly realized it wasn't just a piece of paper. It was a five-by-seven photograph.

Even with heels on, Darby had to stand on her tiptoes for a good view of the picture. In the middle of a large, empty room, a man sat in a chair, his posture stiff and oddly strained. The low quality of the photograph reminded Darby of one of those cheap, do-it-yourself picture-printing machines found in drugstores. She squinted, wishing the exposure wasn't so dark. "He looks familiar."

"You know him?"

"I'm not sure. Maybe."

She reached for the picture but he pulled it back. "Fingerprints," he reminded her, holding the edges with his gloved fingers. When she lowered her hands, he held the picture in front of her.

She tapped her nails against her thigh. "Why would he have his picture taken sitting in the middle of an empty room?"

"That's a concrete floor. And those are industrial-style windows across the back. Probably a warehouse." His jaw tightened. "And he's not sitting there because he wants to." He pointed to the arms of the chair. "He's tied up."

She let out a gasp and leaned closer to get a better look. Recognition slammed into her, stealing her breath. Was this some kind of joke?

"You know him," Rafe said, not a question this time. "Who is he?"

"An attorney, Victor Grant. He used to be in private practice, but he made assistant district attorney last week. I saw him at the courthouse just yesterday."

He set the photograph down to reach for the envelope again. When he pulled out the watch, she realized it didn't have a wristband connected to it. Rafe's eyes widened and he let out a vicious curse. He grasped the watch in one hand and yanked his cell phone out of his jeans pocket with the other.

"What's wrong?" Darby hated the alarm in her voice, but what had seemed like a harmless prank a few minutes ago now seemed like something far more sinister.

Rafe issued rapid-fire instructions into the phone to someone named Buresh. In answer to Darby's earlier question, he held the watch down where she could see it.

A stark, digital readout flashed against the white background, displaying 00:00:15. The last number was decreasing—fourteen…thirteen…twelve. Rafe wasn't holding a watch. He was holding a timer.

And it was counting down.

He ended the call and looked at the timer. The corners of his eyes tightened and his gaze shot to hers. "Time's up."

Boom.

Darby ducked at the loud sound, which seemed to have come from right outside.

Rafe dropped the timer on top of the photograph and rushed to the window to look through the blinds. He turned and headed to the door, but paused in the opening. "Don't touch the evidence. And stay put. Don't go anywhere until I get back."

With his words of warning hanging in the air, he ran out of the office. Too curious to sit and wait, Darby hurried to the window. Normally, she could see the glint of the bright Florida sun sparkling off the Intracoastal Waterway behind the office buildings across the street. But instead she saw a small, dark cloud of smoke rising from one of the warehouses.

Her stomach clenched and her fingers curled around the windowsill. Sirens sounded from a short distance away, getting louder and louder. Images flashed through Darby's mind—the word *boom* on the back of the photograph, that horrible sound. It couldn't be a coincidence that there was smoke rising from the warehouse across the street. Could it?

Rafe had ordered her to stay put, but the bomb, if that's what she had heard, had already gone off. And there was a small crowd gathering outside. As she watched, a police car pulled up. A uniformed officer and a man in a business suit got out and ran toward the warehouse. Rafe met them at the doorway and they went inside.

Several more minutes passed and more police cars arrived. A white van with the words *St. Augustine Police Department* printed on the side pulled up. A man in what Darby believed was a bomb suit was helped out of the back. He hurried through the same doorway where Rafe had gone earlier.

The smoke was clearing, and the only visible damage to the outside of the building was a few broken windows. The police weren't evacuating the area. The growing crowd was still on the street watching. And when the man in the bomb suit came back outside and pulled off his protective gear, Darby knew it must be safe.

Her stomach twisted into knots at the idea that a man she'd spoken to just yesterday might have been hurt—or worse. She couldn't stand here, waiting. She had to know if he was okay.

And whether, somehow, this was her fault.

She headed out her office door. Mindy was staring out the window in the empty reception area since they'd already seen all their clients for the day. She looked up in question when Darby marched past her.

"Dr. Steele… Darby, wait. Detective Morgan said to—"

"Stay put. Yes, I know. You do that," Darby said, still miffed that Mindy had abandoned her with Rafe earlier. "I'll be right back." She opened the door and headed outside.

RAFE USED HIS TWEEZERS to pick up a small bomb fragment and drop it into an evidence collection envelope. Fellow detective and bomb tech, Jake Young, was also on his hands and knees a few feet away in the small warehouse, doing the same thing—picking up pieces of the bomb so the two of them could reassemble it at the police station.

Judging by the shrapnel and bits of threaded pipe they'd already found, there was little doubt this had been a pipe bomb. But to figure out the bomber's identity, Rafe needed to know exactly how the bomb had been constructed. Bomb makers tended to settle on a favorite design and stick with it. The bomb's design was like fingerprints, or DNA.

"Nice of you to dress up for work today."

Rafe glanced up at the sound of his boss's voice. Captain Buresh was just stepping inside the warehouse. Although he was only twenty feet away, it would take him a good half a minute to maneuver through the minefield of debris to reach them.

Rafe peeled off his gloves and set his supplies on the jacket he'd already discarded because of the heat. Without bothering to respond to his boss's teasing about his appearance, Rafe stood to greet him. Buresh knew exactly why Rafe was dressed the way he was, and why he was sorely in need of a haircut and a shave.

Blending in with the local criminal element in some of the rougher areas of town was crucial when trying to establish new contacts—future informants—which had been Rafe's assignment for the past month. If he hadn't been sidetracked by Darby's call, he'd be home right now enjoying a long, hot shower. Or he might have already gotten his hair cut short again, which would have made it much easier to bear the Florida summer heat, especially in this warehouse that captured heat like an oven. He ran the back of his hand across his forehead, wiping off the sweat.

"Bring me up to speed," Buresh said, stopping in front of him.

"The coroner took the vic, or what's left of him, out the back a few minutes ago."

"Was the vic the assistant D.A. you mentioned on the phone?"

"Can't be certain yet, but that would be my bet. There was a wallet in the corner, sheltered from the blast, with Victor Grant's driver's license and credit cards inside."

"Whoever did this wanted us to know the vic's identity."

"Looks that way."

Jake paused with tweezers in hand. "If you're not going to help, get out of my way." His voice carried more irritation than warranted. Jake didn't have much use for Rafe, not since Rafe had survived a brutal home invasion a year ago and his wife hadn't.

Shelby Morgan had been Jake's sister. With the killer still at large, and no one else around to target his anger, Jake blamed Rafe. Rafe wished he had the same patience and empathy for Jake that Darby had shown when talking about her clients blaming her. A year of Jake's insults and snide remarks had frayed Rafe's nerves and temper to the breaking point. The only thing holding him back now was that he knew how much his wife had loved her only sibling.

He pushed those dark thoughts to the back of his mind to focus on the present. Bombings were rare in this small tourist town. And premeditated as this one obviously was, Rafe seriously doubted the bomber was going to stop at just one victim.

The bomber was toying with the police, and Darby, by sending the picture and timer. He'd probably assumed Darby would open her mail early this morning, and that the police would have spent all day futilely trying to find and save the victim. Since she hadn't opened her mail until late in the day, unfortunately the police had never had a chance to search for the victim.

And the bomber hadn't gotten his anticipated thrill out of watching the chase.

That had Rafe worried the bomber might feel cheated, and he might pick another victim sooner than he otherwise would have. Would the bomber send Darby another envelope? Had he fixated on her as his audience, or was she the next intended victim? Rafe stepped away from Jake and led Buresh to the open doorway.

"Did you send someone to Dr. Steele's office to keep an eye on her?"

Buresh nodded. "Daniels is there now. He'll watch the building, make sure no one goes in or out."

A small crowd had gathered at the edge of the warehouse's parking lot. Rafe swore when he recognized a familiar figure behind the police line—Darby Steele. "Too late. What was she thinking coming over here? I specifically told her *not* to."

Across the street, Officer Daniels sat in his police car outside Darby's one-story office building. She must have left right after Rafe had, before Daniels arrived. The woman needed to learn what the term *stay put* meant.

"She shouldn't be out in the open, not until we know why the bomber sent her that envelope," Rafe said.

His boss held his hand in the air, waving for Daniels to join them. "I'll have Daniels take her back to her office. You think she's a target?"

"Possibly, or she's someone the bomber knows and he wants to brag about his accomplishments. Either way, she's central to this case. We'll interview her, see if she knows something she doesn't even realize she knows, then keep an eye on her until we get this guy."

Rafe was about to go back inside to help Jake when he realized Darby wasn't standing where he'd seen her a moment ago. He scanned the crowd, looking for the petite brunette in the baby-blue business suit—the woman who'd tilted his world on a crazy angle earlier. The simple act of grabbing her wrist, of feeling her soft skin beneath his, had sent a zing of awareness slicing through him, straight to his groin.

Which made absolutely no sense, because he didn't even *like* Darby Steele.

Daniels reached Buresh, a smile of greeting on his face. "Hey, Captain, Detective. What's—"

"There she is," Rafe interrupted. "Where's she going?"

She was walking away toward the dock at the end of the street. A man was walking beside her, his head covered with a black baseball cap. The two of them were so close there was almost no sunlight separating them.

An uneasy feeling swept through Rafe. He looked back toward the crowd where Darby had been standing just a moment ago. A large manila envelope was lying on the curb. He clawed for the Glock holstered to his side and jerked his head back toward the dock.

Darby and the man she was with were about

to get into a small, red speedboat, bobbing in the water. Sunlight glinted and Rafe saw what he hadn't seen earlier.

A knife pressed against Darby's side.

He took off running. "That's the bomber," he yelled back over his shoulder. "He's got Darby!"

Chapter Two

The man with the knife shoved Darby into the small boat, making her fall to the floor, scraping her knees against the nonskid fiberglass. Ignoring the flash of pain, she scrambled back to her feet and lunged toward the side to jump in the water and escape.

"Oh, no, you don't." The man grabbed her ankle and yanked hard, making her fall back to the bottom of the boat again.

He crouched over her, pressing the knife against her side. "Try that again and you're dead."

A violent shiver shook Darby. Her breath caught in her throat. The man's eyes were concealed behind a pair of dark sunglasses, and his hair was covered by a Jacksonville Suns baseball cap. But she didn't need to see his eyes to know he wasn't bluffing.

The sharp pain in her side and the warm blood seeping through her clothes told her that.

She nodded, letting him know she understood.

He waved the knife in front of her face in warning, before straightening and grabbing the steering wheel. A quick turn of the key and the engine started. With the practiced ease of someone familiar with boats, he unhooked the nylon lines tying the boat in place. The sound of footsteps pounding against the wooden planks of the dock had him jerking his head up.

Rafe Morgan was sprinting toward them, his arms and legs pumping like an Olympic runner. He was holding a large, black gun in his hand. Far behind him a uniformed police officer was running hard to catch up.

"Police, stop," Rafe yelled. He raised his gun, but didn't shoot.

The man with the knife cursed and moved some levers next to the steering wheel, making the engine whine as the boat pulled away.

Without slowing, Rafe launched himself off the end of the dock, landing in the boat on top of the other man, knocking him back against the bench seat in front of the steering wheel.

Darby barely managed to scramble out of the way before the men fell to the floor on the far side of the bench, wedged between the seat and the side of the boat. They grappled for control of the knife. Darby prayed the blood on the blade was hers, not Rafe's.

Where was his gun? Had he dropped it? No—

there it was, tucked into the holster at his waist. He must have shoved it there just as he leaped off the dock. He'd probably been too worried about hitting her to take a shot.

A sudden rocking motion had Darby staggering back, then slamming into the metal railing at the rear of the boat. She grabbed the railing just before her momentum would have carried her into the water, into the engine's propellers. She shuddered and jerked back, her lungs heaving and her pulse pounding in her ears. She clutched the railing as the boat bumped up and down across the wake of other boats, racing out into the middle of the Intracoastal.

With no one at the wheel.

The two men were locked in a deadly struggle, still wedged between the seat and the side of the boat. Rafe's arm muscles bulged as he tried to wrestle the knife from the other man. Darby wanted to help but she didn't know what to do. The dock was so far away now it was a tiny speck in the distance. And the boat was rocking wildly from side to side, making it impossible to stand.

She crawled forward on her hands and knees toward the other side of the bench. Rafe knocked the knife out of the other man's hand. It flipped over the bench and rattled across the floor of the boat in front of Darby, just as she brought her knee down.

A sharp, burning pain had her jerking back and

biting her lip to keep from crying out. Bright red blood smeared the bottom of the boat beneath her, making it slippery. She fell again, banging her head so hard it brought tears to her eyes. A buzzing noise sounded in her ears, followed by a loud horn.

A loud horn?

She raised her head and her mouth dropped open. A much larger boat was bearing down on them, blasting its horn in warning as its driver turned to avoid them.

"Darby, turn the boat, turn the boat! Hard to port!" Rafe yelled, just before the man he was fighting threw a punch that cracked the detective's head against the side of the boat.

Darby winced and edged around the bench, gasping against the fiery pain in her knee and the throbbing in her side. She reached up for the steering wheel. She had no clue what *port* meant, but she went on instinct, yanking the steering wheel hard left. They turned sharply, missing the other boat by a few feet.

The wake violently rocked the smaller boat and sloshed brackish water over the side, drenching her and the men. Unguided, the boat swerved into one of the dozens of narrow channels leading into the surrounding marsh.

Looking over at the two men, Darby was relieved to see that Rafe's larger size and strength had finally won the fight. The detective pinned the other man facedown and handcuffed his hands behind his back.

Darby turned back around to try to stand so she could steer the boat. She gasped in horror and lunged for the steering wheel.

Too late.

The shallow marsh rushed up to meet them. The hull of the boat hit the muddy ground with a sickening crunch and stuck, tossing the back of the boat skyward. The force of the impact catapulted Darby, Rafe and the other man into the air. Darby screamed and threw her hands out, bracing for impact. She landed with a squishy thud, her momentum rolling her over onto her back. Her head hit the ground so hard she thought she heard her teeth rattle.

She lay for what felt like hours, but was probably only a few minutes, blinking up at the light blue sky above her. A gray-and-white seagull flew overhead, giving a sharp cry as if it were mocking her. Every bone and muscle in Darby's body hurt, from the bottom of her feet to the top of her head. But she took that as a good sign. If she could feel this much pain, at least that meant she was still alive.

The rotten smell of the mud and long brownish-green marsh grass filled her nostrils, making her shiver with revulsion. She gingerly tried to move her arms. Not broken, or at least, she could still move them. She tried to sit up, but the foul-smell-ing mud was like glue, holding her in place. With a great shove, she pushed herself sideways. The mud made a sucking noise, reluctantly releasing its hold. She rolled onto her stomach, gathered her knees beneath her, and tried to push herself up.

A menacing noise had her stomach clenching with dread. She slowly lifted her head, already knowing what she would see. A dull vibrating roar, like a lion, but more ominous and deep, sounded again. Fifteen feet away, directly in front of her, its jaws opened wide as it hissed, was the biggest alligator she'd ever seen.

RAFE ARMY-CRAWLED through the mud and grabbed Darby before she could jerk back and make the gator charge at her. He lay half on top of her, his head pressed next to hers, his left hand clamped over her mouth. Without taking his gaze off the enormous reptile hissing across from them, he whispered, "Don't move."

She gave her head a tiny jerk in what he thought was a nod.

He lowered his hand.

"What do we do?" she whispered.

The fear in her voice had him looking at her face. She was deathly pale beneath the splotches of mud smeared across her skin, but she wasn't falling apart in a sea of tears as he would have expected. She was tougher than she looked.

"I'll have to shoot it," he whispered back, already hating what he had to do. They were both in this gator's territory and she was probably just as scared as Darby.

He snaked his right arm beneath him in the mud to his holster. Empty. He swore. "My gun's gone." He could only hope it was lost in the marsh, not in the hands of the man he'd handcuffed seconds before the crash.

"Can you call for help?" Darby whispered, her terrified gaze locked on the gator.

"My phone's waterlogged. Already tried. How bad are you hurt?"

"I think I can run, if that's your real question."

"Then I guess we're going to run. Not straight, though. That gator is faster than we are, but only in a straight line. We'll have to zigzag to have any chance at outrunning her."

"Her?"

"Most likely. That mound of mud she's on looks like a nest. She's protecting her young."

The gator hissed again, and swished her massive tail as if preparing to charge. Rafe circled his left arm around Darby's waist and braced his right hand beneath him. The gator was too close to give them time to stand and run. This was going to be close, *very* close.

"We're going to roll to the right on the count of

three. No matter what we hit or roll through, keep rolling until I stop you, understand?"

She cringed as the hissing got louder. "Okay," she squeaked, her voice so low he barely heard her.

"One, two, three!" He jerked her out of the mud, rolling her body with his out of the gator's path.

The alligator charged, its snapping jaws narrowly missing Darby. She screamed again and clung to Rafe. He rolled over and over with her clasped to his body until they were a good twenty feet from the gator. He jumped to his feet, lifting her out of the mud and grabbing her hand. The gator turned and came at them again. Rafe yanked Darby's hand and they zigzagged out of the gator's path.

Another hiss and a splash sounded behind them.

Rafe looked back but didn't see the gator anymore. He pulled Darby to the left, just in case, keeping up their zigzagging pattern as they ran through the marsh into the surrounding cover of trees.

"I think we lost her." He slowed since Darby was gasping for breath and struggling to keep up, stumbling every few steps.

She immediately stopped and collapsed onto the ground. "I can't run anymore," she gasped, her chest heaving. "My feet, my…everything." She closed her eyes, drawing in deep, shaky breaths.

Rafe drew a few choppy breaths himself, adrenaline surging through his body. He took a good look around, feeling naked without his gun. He couldn't see the water now. They were deep in the marsh, with spindly oaks and palms surrounding them. But they were still in gator territory, not to mention water moccasin territory. This time of year snakes were in abundance, and could be hiding just about anywhere for an unwary foot to find.

Even more of a worry was the man he'd hand-cuffed. A determined man might be able to contort himself enough to work his cuffed hands over his rear and his legs to get his hands in front of him, which meant he'd be able to use that gun if he found it. Rafe had looked for him right after the crash, but he'd abandoned his search when he heard the gator hissing and realized Darby was in trouble.

He glanced around one more time before crouching next to Darby. She'd mentioned her feet hurt, and he could see why. The high heels she'd been wearing earlier were long gone and the bottoms of her feet were scraped and bleeding. No telling what she'd stepped on while fleeing across the marsh. The mud could hide anything from oyster shells to broken beer bottles. At the very least, she probably needed a tetanus shot.

"I'll carry you. There should be some houses close by." He put an arm around her waist, but she grimaced in pain.

He immediately let her go and gently lifted her suit jacket, frowning at the splotches of blood darkening her side. His hands tightened around the fabric when he saw the straight, deliberate cuts in her white shirt. "That's not from the crash."

Her teeth bit into her bottom lip. "He…cut me, at the warehouse, to get me to move. And again, in the boat."

God help the bomber if Rafe got his hands on him before someone else did. Purposely hurting a woman was at the top of his list of unforgivable sins. He gently pulled the edge of Darby's blouse up to see how badly she was hurt. "The cuts aren't that deep. You'll need a handful of stitches, though."

"I shouldn't have left my office." She winced as he tugged her blouse and jacket back into place. "I should have stayed there like you told me."

"Damn straight you should have stayed."

Her lips thinned and she looked away.

He immediately regretted his harsh words. Until now, he'd never thought of Dr. Darby Steele as anything but a quack with a tendency to ruin his best cases with her so-called expert testimony. But seeing her hurt, and scared, had him feeling like a jerk for raising his voice.

Since she wasn't looking at him, he took full advantage of her inattention to study her. She was far more delicate-looking up close than he'd expected. Her brown hair had fallen free from the severe bun she normally wore, gently curling around her shoulders, making her look softer, more approachable. The jackets she always wore concealed generous curves he wouldn't have known existed if he hadn't pulled the cloth aside to look at her cuts. He'd seen her dozens of times through the years, but this was the first time he'd ever *really* seen her.

And he liked what he saw.

That thought had him stiffening with self-disgust. This was a woman who would say anything to help the defense, and get criminals light, cushy sentences in a mental hospital instead of the tough treatment they deserved in a maximum-security prison.

"Are you hurt anywhere else?" he asked.

She smoothed her muddy, hopelessly ruined skirt. "Nothing serious, I don't think."

Obviously she had other injuries or she would have just said no. "Where else are you hurt?"

He noticed for the first time that her eyes were a light shade of green. What the heck was wrong with him? Why was he noticing the color of her eyes? He dropped his gaze, and that's when he noticed her bloody knees.

"Good grief, woman. You're bleeding everywhere." Her right knee was scraped, nothing serious. But the left…she had a two-inch gash that was trickling blood. "Did he cut you anywhere else?"

"I don't think so." She leaned forward to look at her leg. "It's not that bad, is it?"

"Bad enough." He yanked his shirt up over his head.

"What are you doing?" She sounded alarmed, her eyes widening, her gaze dipping to his chest.

"We have to stop the bleeding." He folded his shirt and held it against the gash on her knee. She blanched and scrunched her eyes shut.

"Hold it tight," he said, grabbing one of her hands and settling it on top of the shirt. "Put as much pressure as you can."

He needed to get her out of here to a hospital. They weren't exactly in the middle of nowhere. There had to be some houses close by, where the marsh ended and prime real estate began.

Shading his eyes against the sun peeking through the trees overhead, Rafe stood and looked around. There, in a break in the trees behind Darby, he could just make out the outline of a building, a few hundred yards away.

"There's a house through those trees. In a couple of minutes we'll have you in an ambulance on the way to the hospital. You're going to be fine."

"I hardly think I need an ambulance. It's not that bad." Her voice was thin and tight, her eyes closed. She was obviously in more pain than she wanted to admit.

And Rafe didn't agree with her assessment of her injuries. That cut on her knee wasn't going to stop bleeding on its own. He bent down to pick her up, then froze at the feel of a gun barrel pressing between his shoulder blades.

Chapter Three

Rafe slowly straightened and put his hands in the air.

"Who are you?" The man behind him shoved the gun against his back. "What are you doing on my property?"

The raspy, older quality of the man's voice reassured Rafe. The bomber had seemed close to Rafe's age, thirty-five, much younger than this man sounded.

"I'm Detective Rafe Morgan with the St. Augustine Police Department. The woman with me is Dr. Darby Steele. We've been in a boating accident and I need to get her to a hospital."

The gun wobbled against his back, as if the man behind him wasn't sure whether or not to believe him. Finally, the gun eased back, and Rafe turned around. The rifle was now pointing at his chest.

"Miss." The old man's eyes didn't leave Rafe as he spoke to Darby. "You okay? Did this man hurt you?"

"No, no, he didn't hurt me. He's a police officer, like he said."

"Hair's a bit long to be a cop." The old man's mouth twisted, his disapproval obvious. "And I doubt they let their officers go without shaving these days, not unless they've gotten pretty darn sloppy."

"I've been working undercover." It wasn't exactly the truth, since the men he'd been grooming as informants knew he was a cop, but it was close enough.

"Uh-huh. Let me guess. You don't have ID with you to prove you're a cop."

"In my back pocket, if my wallet's still there." He started to reach toward his pocket, but the old man's hands tightened on the rifle.

"Look," Rafe said, close to losing his patience, "I don't care if you believe me or not. But Dr. Steele needs medical attention. Do you have a cell phone with you? Call 9-1-1 and tell them to get an ambulance and the police out here. They can verify who I am."

Doubt entered the man's eyes and Rafe thought he might be starting to believe his story, but Rafe didn't have time to wait for the man to make up his mind. Right now the bomber, if he'd survived the crash, could be getting away. Or, he could be waiting in the woods to grab Darby. Staying in one place was too dangerous.

"Are you going to make that call or not?" Rafe prodded.

The man's lips pursed. "I'm thinking about it. I don't have my phone with me in any case. It's back up at the house."

"Darby," Rafe called out without turning around, "I need you to stay down."

"What do you mean?" she asked.

"Don't stand up."

"I'm not standing. I'm still sitting on the—"

Rafe lunged for the man's rifle, shoving the barrel up in the air before yanking the gun from the older man's grip. The man was so startled he just stood there with his mouth hanging open.

"Go on," Rafe ordered. "Get out of here. Make that call."

The man's face paled. He took off in a lumbering gait back toward his house.

Rafe shook his head and turned back to Darby. He swore when he realized that she'd let the shirt drop to the ground during the commotion. Blood was dripping down her calf.

"The shirt, Darby. Press it against the wound."

Her eyes widened and she made a choking sound as she looked past him.

Rafe whirled around.

Too late.

Something hard crashed down on the side of his head. Sharp, fiery pain radiated through his skull and his world went black.

RAFE CRUMPLED TO the ground.

Darby let out a strangled cry. She only had a second to realize the man who'd hit Rafe was the man who'd grabbed her at the warehouse, before he grabbed a fistful of her hair and yanked her up off the ground.

She clawed at his hands, trying to ease the horrible pressure.

He shook her as if in warning and let her fall back to the muddy ground. Sharp, fiery pain knifed through her side. She bit her lip to keep from crying out, clutching her side to stop the bleeding that had started again.

Above her, the man who'd attacked Rafe stood with his handcuffed hands in front of him, wrapped around the grip of a familiar-looking gun. Rafe's gun.

At this range, he couldn't miss.

Time slowed to a crawl. Darby's vision narrowed, everything else fading away except the dark maw of the gun barrel pointing at her. She dug her fingers into the mud beneath her and squeezed her eyes shut, waiting for the shot she knew would come, waiting for death.

"Look at me, stupid witch."

Her eyes flew open. She forced herself to look away from that terrifying gun, at the man standing over her. His baseball cap and sunglasses were gone. The jeans he wore were torn in several places, with smears of blood darkening the blue fabric.

For such a violent man, his face was rather ordinary, not a face that would strike fear into her if she saw him in a crowd. His hair was brown, although that could be because of all the mud packed in it. His eyes were brown, too. So ordinary, and yet, there was nothing ordinary about any of this.

He wasn't looking at her now. Instead, he was squinting toward the trees, where the old man had gone a few minutes ago. Had he heard something? Was someone coming?

Hope flared in Darby's chest. She risked a quick glance at Rafe, lying facedown in the mud a few feet away. He wasn't moving. She couldn't even tell if he was breathing. Was he alive? A sinking feeling shot through her, as if she was on a roller coaster and had just plunged down a steep drop. If he was alive, he wouldn't be for long, not with his face in the mud, blocking his airway. She needed to wipe the mud from his nose and mouth.

She needed a weapon.

She glanced frantically around, searching for the rifle Rafe had been holding. When she saw it, her hopes plummeted. Only three feet away, so close, but impossible to reach because it was behind the gunman. Not that she knew how to use a gun anyway, even if she could somehow get to it without being shot. Her entire body started shaking.

Get it together, Darby. If Rafe is alive, you're his only chance. You have to focus, help him. Somehow.

The gunman's attention snapped back to her, and he took a step forward.

"What do you want?" she choked out past her tightening throat.

"I want these cuffs off," he snarled, shaking the gun, making the cuffs on his wrists rattle against the short chain between them. "Get the key."

"I don't have the key. I don't know where—"

"The cop. Check his pockets."

Yes. Thank God. An excuse to go to Rafe.

She pushed herself up, sucking in a breath at the pain in her side, the sharp burn in her knees. Not sure she had the strength to stand, she crawled to Rafe's still form, using the marshy grass to pull herself forward. When she reached him, she placed herself between him and the shooter so he couldn't see what she was doing. She gently turned Rafe's head to the side and wiped mud away from his nose and mouth.

Breathe. Come on, breathe.

"What are you doing?" The shooter's angry voice was nearly on top of her. "You're wasting time." He cuffed the side of her head with the gun, throwing her against Rafe.

She bit her lip to keep from crying out, but risked one more swipe of her hand over Rafe's mouth, carving out a depression in the mud.

"Get the key, or I'll bust your skull just like his."

His voice held the promise of death. She turned to the side, keeping a wary eye on him.

The sound of sirens in the distance had his mouth contorting with fury. He drew the gun back like a hammer, ready to strike.

"Okay, okay, I'm looking!" Darby dug her hand into Rafe's back pockets, but the only thing she found was his wallet. She tried to roll him over, but he was too heavy. "I have to turn him over to check his front pockets. Help me."

He hesitated, but the sound of sirens seemed to spur him on. He knocked her out of the way and used his foot to shove Rafe onto his back. Motioning her forward with his cuffed hands still wrapped around the gun, this time he aimed at Rafe's head, his grip steady and firm.

"The key. Or the cop dies."

Panic sucked the air from Darby's lungs. She scrambled back to Rafe and shoved her hand in his front left pocket. She pulled out a roll of cash, which the gunman grabbed from her. She shoved her hand back in the same pocket, but it was empty. Moving to his other pocket, she slid her hand inside. Her fingers wrapped around a small chain, with a tiny key on the end. As she pulled out the key, the fingers of Rafe's left hand brushed against her thigh. The movement was so slight, she wasn't sure if she'd imagined it.

Her gaze flew to his face. His eyes were shut, but had his eyelashes fluttered? Was there a new tension in his jaw that hadn't been there before?

A dull thud against her cheekbone had her crying out and sprawling in the mud. Glaring at the gunman, she pushed herself back to a sitting position. The side of her face throbbed in rhythm with her racing pulse.

He raised the gun, ready to hit her again.

She held the key up in the air, shaking it, making the tiny chain dance in the sunlight. "I've got it," she cried. "I've got the key."

He crouched in front of her, pressing the barrel of the gun against her belly. The sirens had stopped now, as if the police had reached their destination. The gunman's eyes took on a feral look. His expression filled with pure hate, and something far more dangerous.

Desperation.

"Unlock the cuffs or I *will* shoot you."

She reached out, grabbing one of the cuffs with one hand, holding the key in the other. Her hands were shaking so hard she almost dropped the key. She bit her lip, concentrating on holding her hands steady. He would shoot her once the cuffs were off. She was sure of it. And then he'd shoot Rafe, lying helpless in the mud.

Stall him. She had to do something to get him to turn the gun away from her. She fumbled with the key, this time on purpose. "I can't...get it. You're too close. I can't get leverage."

A shout sounded from the woods, but Darby couldn't make out the words.

The gunman jerked the gun to the side, moving back a foot to give her room.

Darby weighed her options. How close were the police? If she waited, would they make it in time to save Rafe? To save her?

As if reading her mind, the gunman turned his gun toward Rafe again.

"Here!" She shoved the key in the lock, wiggling it until she heard a loud click. She unlocked the second cuff and it popped open. The gunman twisted the cuffs off his wrists and dropped them to the ground.

"Detective Morgan?" a voice called out from the woods nearby.

"Dr. Steele? Are you out here?" Another voice, followed by the sound of branches snapping and leaves rustling.

"Time to die." The gunman pointed the gun back toward Darby.

Oh, God. She squeezed her eyes tightly shut and waited.

A shot rang out, an explosion of sound that made Darby whimper and cover her ears. She waited for the pain, but it never came. The sound of grunts and cursing had her opening her eyes.

Rafe was on top of the gunman. The two men were locked in a struggle for the gun.

Darby scrambled back out of the way and yelled for the police. "Over here! Help us!"

Two officers crashed through the trees toward them.

The gunman twisted violently, smashing the gun into Rafe's jaw. Rafe cursed and fell to the side. With the pistol in hand, the gunman lunged to his feet, snatched up the rifle and took off running toward the marsh.

Rafe tried to get up, but fell back down, holding his head.

Darby scrambled to him just as the policemen reached them.

"Are you Dr. Steele?" one of them asked. The other officer ran after the gunman.

"Yes. Please help us! Detective Morgan needs an ambulance."

Rafe shook her off and staggered to his feet. "She's the one who needs the ambulance. Give me your gun."

"Detective, I'm not sure that's a good—"

"Your gun. Now."

The officer handed him his gun. Rafe took off in an unsteady line through the trees.

"What are you doing?" Darby cried out. She glared at the policeman above her. "Go on. Help him!"

"Sorry, ma'am, but I'm not leaving you alone out here. I'll wait for backup."

No amount of arguing would make the policeman leave her and go help Rafe. Darby stared in frustration at the gap in the trees where Rafe had disappeared.

A few minutes later the marsh was crawling with cops. One of them insisted on carrying Darby to the waiting ambulance. She'd wanted to wait for Rafe to come back, but the policeman wouldn't listen. She felt silly being carried, especially since the officer should be out helping Rafe instead of worrying about her.

Where was Rafe? Was he okay? No one seemed to know the answer to that question, and soon she was in the back of the ambulance being rushed to Flagler Hospital a short distance away.

In spite of all the blood, her injuries weren't life threatening. While the emergency room doctor stitched up her knee, a police officer took her statement and her description of the suspect.

"Have you heard anything about Detective

Morgan?" she asked. "Is he okay? Did he catch the gunman?"

"I don't know anything about that, Dr. Steele," the officer replied.

She dug her fingers into the crinkly paper covering the examining room table.

"Worried about me, huh?"

Rafe! He stood in the doorway between two uniformed officers. He was shirtless and smeared with mud. Darby's relief turned to concern when she saw how pale and unsteady he was. It looked as if the only reason he wasn't falling down was because the policemen were holding on to his arms.

The doctor taking care of Darby pressed a last piece of tape into place on her leg and hurried to Rafe.

"Sit him down over here. He should have been brought in on a gurney. What happened?"

"Gurneys are for sissies." Rafe's words were slurred. As soon as he sat on the examining table the doctor pointed to, he fell backward with a groan.

DARBY YAWNED AND STRETCHED, her muscles aching from being scrunched into the uncomfortable chair in Rafe's hospital room where she'd fallen asleep. The clock on the wall facing his bed showed it was twenty minutes until midnight.

His face was relaxed in sleep. He looked far less

intimidating and more approachable now that he wasn't wearing his usual frown. She wished he would wake up. The doctors had said he'd fully recover, but she needed to look him in the eyes and hear his impatient voice for herself. The man might be infuriating most of the time, but he'd risked everything for her. She needed to thank him for saving her life.

A light knock sounded on the door. Before Darby could fully rise from her chair, Captain Buresh walked into the room, waving her back down.

"Don't get up." His voice was pitched low, barely above a whisper. "What are you doing in here? You aren't supposed to be roaming the halls."

"Since my room is next door, I don't think you can accuse me of roaming the halls. There'd be no point anyway, since there's no one else to talk to. What did you do, clear out an entire hospital wing just for the two of us?"

"Moving the other patients to another floor was a security measure."

"For Rafe and me, or for the other patients?"

He shrugged. "I'd feel better for everyone if you stayed in your room, under guard."

"I *am* under guard. I'm sure you noticed Officer Daniels outside."

He sighed as if he was too tired to argue, and stepped closer to the bed. "Has he woken up yet?"

Darby pushed her aching body out of the chair

and stood across from him, on the other side of the bed. In addition to the hospital gown she was wearing, she had a second one she was using as a robe. She self-consciously pulled it tighter around her. "He hasn't been awake since I came in here. The doctor said he has a slight concussion, that he can go home tomorrow if all goes well."

Buresh nodded, reminding Darby that he probably already knew the details about Rafe's condition. He was, after all, his boss. She glanced at the wall clock again. "Why are you here so late?"

"I...ah...wanted to check on you and Detective Morgan before I went home. It's been a long day, and I needed to put my mind at ease before trying to get some sleep."

Did the hesitation in his voice mean there was more to what he was saying—or rather, what he *wasn't* saying?

"Have you caught him yet?" Rafe's raspy voice called out from the bed. His eyes were open now. He pressed the buttons on the railing, raising himself into a sitting position.

Darby handed him the cup of water on the rolling tray, figuring he was probably as thirsty as she'd been earlier, in spite of the IV. She hadn't given much thought to the heat when she'd been fighting for her life in the marsh, but afterward, she'd felt like a wilted flower, dry as dust.

He gave her a grateful nod and took a long sip before handing the cup back to her. "Are you all right?"

"The doctor wants me to stay overnight to make sure I don't develop an infection from getting all that nasty swamp mud in my cuts, but overall, no worse for wear." She studied him closely. "How do *you* feel?"

"Fine for someone who can't remember how he got knocked out. What happened? The doctor had no clue."

Buresh exchanged a startled glance with Darby.

"You don't remember?" Buresh asked.

"I remember the boat, the alligator and some old man holding a rifle on me. Everything else is a big blank until I was in the ambulance."

"Retrograde amnesia," Darby said.

Rafe narrowed his eyes at her. "I don't have amnesia. I remember what happened…most of it." His scowl was as fierce as Darby had ever seen it, which was saying quite a bit.

"It's nothing to be embarrassed about," she said. "It's normal with head trauma. You forget what happened before the event that caused the injury. I've seen my share of clients in therapy with similar problems. Since you remember most of what happened before you got knocked out, you've got an excellent chance of regaining all of your memory."

He didn't look as though he appreciated her analysis. He was a big guy, more than capable of

taking care of himself and those around him—
normally. It had to be a blow to his ego to think
he'd been knocked out and unable to help her, especially given his past, when he'd been knocked
unconscious, unable to protect his wife in a home
invasion. That reminder had Darby groaning inside.
Great. She should have just kept her mouth shut.

"It doesn't matter," Buresh said, filling the awkward silence. "The few minutes you lost wouldn't
have added anything to the investigation. Dr. Steele
gave a statement and a description of the bomber.
She was an excellent eyewitness."

Rafe winced and pressed a hand against his tem-
ple.

The corners of Buresh's eyes crinkled with concern. "You need me to get the doctor?"

"I'm fine," Rafe gritted out. "You never answered my question. Have you caught the bomber?"

"Not yet." Buresh gave Rafe a brief summary
of what had happened after Rafe was knocked unconscious, and the progress of the ongoing search.
Buresh glanced uneasily at Darby, hesitating. "The
envelope the bomber left at the warehouse had another timer and a photograph inside."

"Who was in the picture?" Rafe asked.

Buresh looked at Darby.

A shiver of fear sliced through her. *This* was
what Buresh had been hiding earlier, why he'd hes-

itated when he'd first come into the room. "It was a picture of me, wasn't it?"

He sighed in surrender. "Yes."

She rubbed her hands up and down her suddenly chilled arms.

"And the timer?" Rafe asked.

"The timer runs out at midnight." Buresh's voice was awkward, low.

Rafe and Darby both looked at the clock on the far wall. Ten minutes until midnight. Darby swallowed hard.

"We've searched half the marsh," Buresh continued. "But at this point, I don't hold out much hope of finding him there. We've been performing door-to-door searches to rule out that he entered someone's house or took hostages. So far, nothing."

"Loan me your gun while I'm in here," Rafe said. "I don't feel right without one."

Buresh was shaking his head even before Rafe finished. "I'm not leaving a gun with a man with a concussion. Who would keep an eye on it when you're sleeping? And I'm certain the nurses wouldn't appreciate finding it under your pillow when they change the sheets."

Rafe didn't look happy with his captain's refusal.

Darby tapped the bed rail. "You're sure the bomber's not…in the hospital, right?" She let out an uneasy laugh.

Buresh gave her a reassuring smile. "You're

completely safe here, Dr. Steele. I've got an officer posted in the emergency room. That's the only
access to the hospital this time of night. And Officer Daniels will stand guard until morning, when
another officer takes his place."

Her doubt must have shown on her face, because
he gave her an admonishing look, as if he was disappointed that she didn't trust him. "Half the police force is looking for the man who abducted you.
He's on the run. He wouldn't have a chance to follow through on his 'midnight' threat, even if he
knew where you were—which he doesn't."

"It can't be difficult to figure out where I am,
Captain," she said. "There's only one hospital in
the area, and he knew I was hurt."

The captain's face reddened. "Not true, Dr.
Steele. We could have taken you into Jacksonville.
Baptist Medical Center South is just a short drive
up the interstate."

Darby regretted her reply. She hadn't meant to
sound sarcastic, but obviously Buresh had taken
it that way.

"Regardless," he said, "you're safe here. What
I'm worried about is what happens after you leave
the hospital. Until we catch this man, we have to
assume you're still a target." He glanced at Rafe.
"You'll need to be on light duty for a few days, so
I have the perfect assignment for you. I want you

to watch over Dr. Steele until we have the bomber in custody."

Rafe shook his head. "I'm not a babysitter, and you can't afford to have your best detective on the sidelines right now."

Darby tapped her nails on the railing again to get Rafe's attention. "I don't need a babysitter. But I *would* appreciate having an experienced police officer nearby. It would make me feel much safer. And I promise I won't get in your way."

"This isn't a debate," Buresh said. "When you're both discharged tomorrow, you're going into hiding, together. End of discussion."

Darby wrinkled her brow. "Into hiding? Wait a minute. I thought I'd have police protection, but that I'd be able to go back to work. My clients book appointments months in advance. I can't just cancel without notice."

Rafe frowned at her. "If you go back to your office, you'll put your clients—and Mindy—at risk. Buresh is right about one thing. You do need protection." He turned back to Buresh. "But I'm not the one who'll be protecting her."

"We'll talk more about this in the morning," Buresh said. "I suggest you both get some sleep. Dr. Steele, would you like me to walk you back to your room?"

"No, thank you. I'd like to talk to Detective Morgan before I go."

"All right. Good night, then." He turned and left.

"It's not personal, you know," Rafe said.

Darby tightened her fingers around the bed railing. "You sure about that?"

"I wouldn't want to pull guard duty for *anyone,* regardless of my opinion about what they did for a living. I have more important things to do, like finding the man who killed the A.D.A., the man who almost killed you."

Her stomach tightened at the reminder that someone she knew had actually been murdered today, and how close both she and Rafe had come to being the bomber's next victims. "I know you aren't exactly a fan of mine. I can live with that. But I still wanted to thank you. You saved my life. You were almost killed." She swallowed hard. "No one has ever…" She was about to say *cared,* but that wasn't the right word.

She cleared her throat and tried again. "No one has ever *fought* for me like that. And you shouldn't have had to. If I'd followed your instructions, stayed at my office, none of this would have happened. You wouldn't be lying in this bed right now."

Without stopping to think about what she was doing, she reached out and put her hand on his. His face mirrored his surprise, but when she would have snatched her hand back, he entwined his fingers with hers. Maybe it was exhaustion, maybe it was just that she was tired of fighting and was tired of feeling so alone, but when his hand wrapped around hers, she held on tight.

"If you'd followed my instructions, you'd be dead," he said.

She blinked in surprise. "What? What do you mean?"

"If you'd stayed in your office, the bomber could have abducted you out the back door. We only had one policeman watching your building, from the front, because none of us really thought the bomber would strike again so soon. I thought one cop was enough of a deterrent, but I don't believe that now. Not after everything that happened. The only reason you're here right now, alive, is because you were too stubborn to 'stay put.' So, no apologies necessary. I'm glad you didn't do what I told you to do."

She drew a deep breath to hold off the unexpected rush of moisture in her eyes. "Thank you."

"You're welcome. But, for the record, if I tell you to do something again, I expect you to do it."

Now, this was what she'd expected. She tugged her hand out of his grasp. "For the record, since you're refusing to be my 'babysitter,' I don't guess it matters what orders you give me, does it?"

The corner of his mouth quirked up. "No, I guess it doesn't."

She twisted her hands together, feeling the loss of his warmth far more than the air-conditioned room warranted. "Well, thank you again, for everything." She glanced up at the clock and grinned. "It's midnight and nothing happened. I guess your boss was right." She covered a yawn. All the stress of the day was catching up to her, and she was looking forward to a good night's sleep. She gave him a wave and headed toward the door.

The lights flickered, followed by a dull boom in the distance. Darby froze and whirled around to look at Rafe.

He was already sliding out of bed when the lights went out.

Chapter Four

The emergency lights popped on, casting a dim yellow glow through Rafe's hospital room. He ripped the tape off his arm and pulled out the IV needle that anchored him to the pole beside the bed.

Darby rushed to his side. "What are you doing? You're bleeding." She grabbed some tissues from a box by the bed and pressed them against his arm.

He grabbed her hands and tugged her to the bathroom doorway beside the bed. "Wait in here," he whispered.

"It's just a power outage, right?" She sounded as if she was trying to convince herself. Her teeth bit into her bottom lip while her eyes practically begged him to agree with her.

He wished he could. He wished he could erase the fear in her eyes. But he already knew the worst had happened.

The bomber had found them.

"Hide in the bathroom, Darby. *Please.*"

She looked as though she was about to protest, but instead, she ran into the bathroom.

Rafe moved to the main door as quietly as he could. He started to bend down to look under the door when a wave of dizziness forced him to brace his hands against the wall. He closed his eyes and willed the room to stop spinning.

"It's the concussion."

His eyes flew open. Darby was standing beside him in her cleverly constructed outfit of two lime-green hospital gowns, one tied in the front, one in the back. He hadn't even given a thought to the flimsy gown covering him. Darby had probably gotten a generous view of his backside when he'd jumped out of bed. He'd laugh if he wasn't so worried right now, and if it wouldn't make his head hurt worse.

"I told you to stay—"

"In the bathroom, I know," she whispered. "But then I thought about your concussion." She glanced at the closed door, her face pale. "Do you want me to open it?"

"No." He winced at how loud his voice sounded in the quiet room. "No," he repeated, in a quieter voice. "I need to know what's on the other side of that door *without* opening it, just in case..."

She visibly swallowed, and nodded, letting him know she understood.

"Unfortunately," he continued, "since I don't have a mirror, I'm going to have to bend down and—"

"Wait." She put her hand on his, stopping him when he started to lower himself to the floor to look under the door. "Give me a second." She hurried to the rolling tray by the bed, the one that held the water pitcher and plastic cup she'd given him to drink out of earlier. She pressed something on the sides, and the tray rolled back to reveal a compartment. She reached inside, tugged on something he couldn't see, then snapped out a rectangular mirror attached to a piece of plastic the same color as the tray.

She held up her prize and hurried back to him. "Voilà."

He squeezed her hand in thanks and took the mirror. "Remind me to arrest you later for destruction of hospital property."

The answering grin on her face faded when he crouched and placed the mirror flat on the floor, sliding it just under the edge of the door. The dim emergency lights in the hallway showed no one was standing outside. What he could see of the hallway was deserted.

It shouldn't have been.

Officer Daniels should have been outside.

A nurse should have been sitting at the nurses' station.

The phone by the bed rang. Darby let out a startled yelp. Her eyes widened in dismay and she clapped her hands over her mouth.

Rafe pulled her to the bathroom again, pushing her inside. He grabbed the phone before it could ring again. "Detective Morgan."

"It's Buresh. Dr. Steele, is she—"

"She's fine. Daniels isn't here, though, and the power's out. What's going on?" He stretched out the phone cord so he could stand closer to the door and watch for any movement reflected in the mirror.

"Something happened to the power transformer. I'm downstairs with Daniels, in the emergency room. He came down to check on the noise. Keep Dr. Steele with you until we get this figured out, okay? SOP, you got that?"

Rafe's fingers tightened around the phone. "Got it. SOP. Call me back once you have more information."

"Will do."

He pressed the button to end the call. Then he dialed 9-1-1. He gave his name, location, and told the operator that an officer needed assistance. Without waiting for a reply, he pitched the phone on the bed, grabbed Darby's hand and pulled her toward the door at a near run.

"What are you doing?" she gasped as he tugged her into the hallway. "What's going on?"

"Be quiet." He squeezed her hand to soften his words. The neon green emergency-exit sign glowed at the end of the hall, drawing him forward like a beacon. All he had to do was get through that door and down the stairs. From there he could get Darby out of the hospital and take her somewhere safe.

A muted noise sounded behind them. Footsteps, coming toward the double doors that blocked off this wing. The exit was still thirty feet away.

Too far.

Rafe shoved the nearest door open and pulled Darby inside the room with him. A brief glance at her face had him wincing. Her complexion was ghostly white, her eyes wide and searching. With good reason.

They were in a world of trouble here.

Easing the door shut, he dropped her hand and did a quick survey of the room. It was another patient's room, thankfully empty because—as the doctor had told Rafe earlier—Captain Buresh had cleared out the floor to keep Darby safe.

Not that his plan had worked.

Footsteps sounded down the hallway again, quiet—as if someone was trying not to make any noise—and stopping and starting, like someone was searching each room, one by one.

Rafe had to do something, fast. He ran to the window and looked out. A three-or four-story drop to the parking lot. No balcony. And there weren't any other exits from this room. He did what he'd been trained to do long ago at the police academy—look up—because most people don't. When he spotted the acoustic tiles in the ceiling above him, he realized exactly what he had to do.

"Rafe," Darby whispered, "what's going on? Wasn't that Buresh on the phone? What did he say?"

He let out a quick breath. "A transformer blew. The captain said he and Daniels were in the E.R. He said we should stay in my room and wait for him to call back."

"Then why did we leave your room?" Her voice was panicked, high-pitched.

He held a finger to her lips, reminding her to whisper. "Because Buresh said Daniels was with him."

"I don't understand." She remembered to whisper this time, but her voice shook with each word. "What does that have to do with—"

He waved her to silence again and crossed to the door. He put his ear against the wood, listening. Nothing, then…another shuffle, a shoe scraping across tile. Whoever was searching the rooms was maybe halfway down the hall. How many doors had he and Darby passed on their sprint from his room? Ten on each side, eleven? Twenty-two rooms to search. Not a lot when there was practically nowhere to hide in each room, other than under the bed or in the bathroom, maybe in the small closet behind each door.

They were running out of time.

He rushed back to her and tried to explain. "Daniels was assigned to guard you," he whispered. "When the lights went out, he should have immediately gone into my room to check on you. That's SOP, standard operating procedure." He looked up again, mentally measuring the height of the ceiling. He could easily lift Darby up there. But how would he follow her up? He didn't want to prop any furniture beneath the hole where they climbed up. That would be like a sign telling the bomber exactly where they were.

"Should we call Buresh back?" Darby asked. "Maybe he forgot about this SOP thing."

"He didn't forget, and there's no point in calling him back," he answered, only half paying attention to the conversation. There, the bathroom door. If he pulled it closed, and braced his foot on the handle, then used the top of the doorframe for leverage, he might be able to pull himself up into the ceiling.

"Why not?" Darby's voice broke on the last word.

Rafe forced himself to focus on what she was asking. "Buresh can't help us, neither can Daniels."

"Why not? Why can't they help us?"

"Because, by now, they're both dead."

DARBY STARED AT RAFE in horror. He'd just told her two police officers were dead, and now he was calmly holding out his hand, telling her to climb on his shoulders so he could lift her into the ceiling?

The man was insane. And he was asking her to do the impossible.

Climb into that black hole where he'd removed the ceiling tile.

The thought of going into that dark space, being cramped between the roof and the flimsy network of railings holding the tiles in place, had her stomach churning with nausea.

"Darby, we have to go now."

She shook her head and backed up a step. She drew in a choppy breath, then another, and risked a quick glance up. No, she wouldn't do it.

She couldn't.

Rafe frowned and dropped his hand. "What's wrong?"

"I just…can't…I can't go up there. I can't." She ran to the door.

Rafe grabbed her before she could open it. "We can't go out in the hall," he whispered furiously, his blue eyes blazing at her. "He's armed. I'm not. It's too risky. Our only chance is to go through the ceiling, but only if we do it *now*."

"We can call Buresh. Maybe you're wrong about him."

"Buresh told me to follow SOP. That was his way of warning me he was under duress. If he could help us, don't you think he'd be here by now?"

He didn't wait for her answer. He pulled her toward the end of the room beneath the opening in the ceiling. "We could wait here for help, but I'm not going to bet my life, or yours, that help will arrive in time."

As Darby stared at the small dark hole in the ceiling, her world began to spin. Black dots swirled in front of her eyes and she had to sit on the floor to catch her breath.

Rafe crouched beside her, a look of surprised understanding on his face. "You're afraid of the dark, aren't you?" His voice sounded incredulous. "Who would have thought a psychologist would be afraid of the dark?"

She stared at the floor, deeply embarrassed. "It's not just the dark. I'm not…comfortable…in tight spaces." She didn't dare look at him again. She knew what she'd see—the same condemnation she'd seen in his eyes the last time they'd crossed proverbial swords in a courtroom.

"Okay, we'll do it your way."

She looked up, certain she couldn't have heard him right.

"I may not understand your fear, but I can see it's real. We'll figure out another way." His brows drew down. "If we have to go through the door, we'll go through the door. We'll have to work our way down the hall, one room at a time, until we get to the exit. But our timing will have to be perfect.

We'll have to run into the hall each time the gunman goes into a room, so he doesn't see us. And we can't make any noise."

Darby remembered the way her own hospital room door had squeaked when she'd opened it to go to Rafe's room. What if one, or more, of the doors they had to go through squeaked, too? The gunman would hear it. They'd be trapped.

She watched in silence as Rafe crossed to the tray that had been beside the bed before he'd moved the bed to block the door. He snapped off the mirror, just like she'd done in the other room. He hurried to the door and got down on his hands and knees, wincing but not slowing down even though his head was obviously hurting. He slid the mirror under the edge of the door.

The man had almost been killed protecting her. And yet, here he was, willing to put himself at risk again even though he felt there was a safer option.

All because of her stupid fear of dark, tight spaces.

Fisting her hands beside her, she forced herself to look up at the ceiling. That dark opening wasn't a hole. She couldn't think of it that way. No, it was an escape hatch. And the tiles surrounding the hole were just, what? Some kind of foam board? Rafe had already explained they were just going to crawl across the beams that supported the ceiling, not across the grid holding up the tiles. The grid wasn't strong enough to support them. If she panicked, and had to get out, all she had to do was drop through one of the tiles. It wasn't as if she'd really be trapped.

There weren't any musty, cold stone walls up there.

Or water dripping all around her.

Or the scurrying of rats as they brushed against her in the dark.

She shivered and clenched her teeth together.

This wasn't a well.

She wasn't a scared little girl again, trapped, waiting, crying for help. She wouldn't have to pull herself up the wet, slimy walls, inch by inch, grasping for holds on rocks that cut her fingers until they bled.

She glanced down at the tiny white lines on her fingers, lines that would never let her forget. She fisted her hands together.

This wasn't a well.

Muted footsteps sounded in the hallway, louder, closer.

Darby's gaze flew to Rafe.

He was motionless by the door, staring into the mirror. He stiffened and jerked back, noiselessly pulling the mirror back inside the room. When he turned toward her, and she saw the grim look on his face, she knew what she had to do.

She had to climb into that hole.

WHAT RAFE HAD SEEN in the hallway was the dark silhouette of the gunman, holding the gun with practiced ease in front of him, far closer to their room than Rafe had expected.

He cursed Buresh beneath his breath for not leaving him a weapon.

Using some oxygen tubing he'd pilfered from a drawer beside the bed, he finished securing his hospital gown tightly against his waist. It made more sense to completely strip the gowns off both him and Darby, so the cloth wouldn't hang down and get in their way when they climbed through the ceiling. But Darby had been so horrified when he'd suggested it that he'd settled for tying their gowns using oxygen tubing and the telephone cord.

After lifting Darby up into the ceiling, Rafe pulled himself up after her and settled on top of a crossbeam. A noise sounded from below, a whisper of sound.

Rafe hurried to secure the tile back in the ceiling. "Come on," he whispered against Darby's ear. "This way." The tiny gaps between the ceiling tiles and the railings allowed enough light in for him to plan their escape route. He could see the end of the hallway thirty feet away. If he could get Darby to that wall, they could drop down into the stairwell.

Halfway to his goal, he glanced back and realized Darby hadn't followed him. She was still crouched on her hands and knees exactly where she'd been when he'd lifted her into the ceiling. He motioned for her to join him, but she didn't react. Her eyes were open but even though she was staring at him, she didn't seem to see him.

Carefully turning around on the beam, he went back to her. There wasn't any sound from the room below. Was the gunman still there? If Darby had followed him across the beam, they'd already be over another room by now, and it wouldn't matter.

Rafe leaned down close to Darby's face. Her eyes were glassy and she was motionless, like a statue. Pressuring her to climb into the ceiling had been a mistake. Her fears were far more serious than he'd realized. Somehow he had to get through to her, to bring her back.

He gently brushed her hair out of her eyes, ran his fingers across her warm, soft skin. No reaction, just that scary, glassy stare. He couldn't even risk whispering to her with the gunman below.

Come on, Darby. Look at me. See me. You can do this.

Her body started to shake. She let go of the beam beneath her and wrapped her arms around her waist. Rafe grabbed for her, barely catching her before she could fall. If he let her go now, she'd fall sideways right through the ceiling tiles, right into the shooter's line of sight.

A noise sounded below. The creak of the bathroom door opening.

Darby's eyes widened, and she let out a low moan.

Rafe did the only thing he could do. He clamped his mouth down on hers to stifle the sound.

The response was intense, immediate.

But not from Darby.

Rafe's pulse kicked into high gear. Blood pumped away from his brain to another part of his anatomy. As if his hand had a life of its own, it spanned down her back, cupping her bottom.

It had been a long time since he'd held a woman. That was the reason he suddenly wanted to tear off Darby's ridiculous and completely adorable hospital gowns. That was the reason he wanted to trace his tongue down the curve of her neck, taste the salty sweetness of her skin.

But that wasn't going to happen. Not with a gunman below. And certainly not when the woman whose lips were pressed against his didn't even know he was there.

He started to pull back, but Darby followed. She leaned forward, her lips parted as she reached her hands up and pulled him back toward her. That was all the encouragement he needed. He thrust his tongue into her mouth, delighted when she moved against him in response. She sucked lightly on his tongue, and his body throbbed against her softness.

She jerked back, and Rafe had to grab her arms to keep her from falling off the beam. Her wide eyes stared at him in horror, as if being held by him was the worst thing that had ever happened to her.

That horrified look was like a bucket of ice water, and suddenly he was just as horrified as she was. How could he have gotten so wrapped up in her that he'd completely forgotten about the gunman?

Her eyes flashed at him and she pushed him away, holding on to the beam again. She looked as if she was ready to give him a furious lecture.

He clamped his hand over her mouth. He looked down toward the room below, then back at her, until her eyes widened with understanding. He slowly eased the pressure of his hand against her mouth, then held a finger in front of his lips, letting her know to be quiet.

When she nodded, he half turned on the beam and pointed to the far end, waving for her to follow him.

She blinked as if only just then realizing where they were. When she didn't move, he grabbed hold of the beam above his head, and maneuvered himself until he was sitting on the beam behind her. He reached down and caressed her bottom. The moment his hand touched her, she jerked and began to crawl across the beam toward the far wall. He gritted his teeth, not at all flattered that she found his touch so distasteful.

Her fears froze her in place twice again, and each time, he ran his hand lightly across her bottom, shocking her into moving forward. By the time they reached the wall, he was hard and aching. This was a heck of a place and time for him to realize that Dr. Darby Steele had a smoking-hot rear end.

At the far wall, she clung to one of the cross-beams, her eyes closed, her entire body shaking.

Sympathy curled inside him. Something terrible must have happened to give her such a deep-seated fear of dark, enclosed places. He pressed his lips next to her ear. "I'm sorry. I shouldn't have pushed you to climb into this ceiling. But it's almost over now. All we have to do is drop down onto the stairwell landing and we're home free. Okay?"

And just like that, she was gone again. She'd retreated back inside herself, her mind blocking out her fears, taking her to a place where she was safe.

Rafe listened intently. He hadn't heard any sounds from below, or any creaking doors opening again, as he and Darby had worked their way across the beam. He hated going down into the stairwell blind, but he wasn't about to sit and wait for gunfire to come strafing up from below, either. They were far too vulnerable and exposed up here.

Curling his fingers around the ceiling tile directly beneath the beam he was sitting on, he quietly lifted it. The landing below was all clear. But there wasn't anything for him to use to climb down. He would have to lower Darby down first, then drop down after her.

He pulled her onto his lap. She didn't react. She just gave him that same glassy stare she'd had before. He scooted forward and braced his legs on two crossbeams, with the opening in the ceiling centered between his thighs.

"I'm going to lower you down into the light," he whispered. "No more dark, tight places, okay?"

She didn't even blink.

Blowing out a frustrated breath, he cradled her in his arms and held her over the hole. He gently released her legs, then held her under her arms, carefully lowering her. He bent down as far as he could, sliding his hands to her biceps, then her forearms, until her feet were dangling just a few inches off the floor. Still, she didn't move. Her breath came in short, choppy pants.

He hated to just let her go, but he had no choice. He released her hands, grimacing when she crumpled onto the concrete landing. He swung out over the opening and dropped down beside her, praying he hadn't hurt her by letting go.

He started to pick her up when the door to the landing flew open. He shoved Darby behind him as a man stepped through the opening, gun in hand, pointed straight at him.

Jake.

Rafe sagged with relief. Had he and Darby been running from a fellow police officer this entire time?

"I'm sure glad it's you." Rafe grinned, but his

smile faded when Jake remained silent and continued to point the gun at him.

"Jake?"

The sound of booted feet clomping up the stairs sounded from below. Jake and Rafe both looked over the railing. The SWAT team had finally arrived.

Jake gave Rafe an odd look, then holstered his gun. "Detectives Jake Young and Rafe Morgan are up here," he called out. "This floor is clear."

The SWAT team stopped on the landing. "We'll do a sweep, just to be sure. We've cleared the lower floors." He looked at Darby. "Is she okay? Does she need a medic, sir?"

Rafe scooped Darby into his arms. "I'll take her to the E.R. and have her checked out."

"Officer Terry will escort you to the elevator on the next level down, sir, while we sweep this floor."

Jake and the SWAT officer led the way down the stairs to the next landing.

The SWAT leader held the door open.

Jake's mouth tightened as Rafe approached him with Darby cradled to his chest. Jake glanced at Darby, then jerked to the side to allow Rafe to pass.

Rafe wasn't sure what to make of his brother-in-law's reaction, but he didn't have time to think about it now. He needed to get Darby help. The SWAT officer led him down the long hallway, through the double doors to the bank of elevators.

Rafe stepped inside the nearest one and punched the button for the first floor.

As the doors began to close, Jake stepped in front of the elevator, his eyes intent, his hands clenched into fists. Rafe didn't bother holding the door for him.

Chapter Five

Dawn was still a few hours away, which had Rafe itching to leave the hospital. He wanted to get Darby out of here, into hiding, before the bomber came looking for her. But he couldn't do that until the doctors cleared her to leave.

She wasn't critical, and wouldn't even be in the intensive care unit except that Rafe had insisted. She'd woken up from that trance almost as soon as he got her to the E.R., which was a huge relief. But a psychiatrist was in with her now. And since the walls in the ICU patient rooms were all glass, this was the perfect place to watch over her, even though Rafe was currently standing in another patient's room directly across the hall—Captain Buresh's room. Buresh had proved to be harder to kill than Rafe had given him credit for.

"I thought you were here to see me, but I guess I was wrong." Buresh's voice sounded weak but amused.

Rafe dragged his gaze back to Buresh. "About time you woke up. You look like hell."

"You don't look so great yourself. The way you're frowning, I expect you still have a devil of a headache. And you look like you're ready to fall down from exhaustion."

"I'm fine."

Buresh snorted. "I bet the doctors disagree with you."

Rafe didn't bother to respond. Buresh knew him well enough to know he wasn't one to follow doctor's orders. He grabbed a plastic chair from across the room and dragged it over to the bed. He straddled the chair and rested his arms across the back. "I've heard a few of the details, but I want your version. What happened after you left my room last night?"

Buresh's hands fisted against the sheets. "You heard about Daniels?"

"I heard he was killed, yes."

A look of pain flashed across Buresh's face. "It's my fault. I didn't post enough officers here at the hospital. I figured the bomber would go to ground, that he wouldn't risk showing himself again so soon with half the police force searching for him."

Having gone through his own blame game for the past year, Rafe understood his boss's guilt all too well. Nothing Rafe could say would make him feel better. Only time would do that. And even then, there would still be moments when the past would slam into him so hard it would steal his breath. He'd relive every agonizing moment of what had happened. Fear would twist his gut, make him wake up in a cold sweat. Rage would pulse through him, making him clench his fists so hard his nails cut into his hands and made him bleed. But no matter how many times he replayed the past in his mind, the result was still the same.

Because no one can change the past.

No matter how desperately they wished they could.

"You want me to come back later?" Rafe asked.

Buresh shook his head and let out a deep sigh. "Waiting won't change anything. Might as well tell you the details while they're still fresh." He scrubbed a hand over his face. "Apparently the bomber stole a lab coat from a doctor's car in the parking lot. When a couple of ambulances pulled up to the E.R., he walked right in. In the confusion, no one noticed an extra doctor walking around."

He absently toyed with the IV tubing by his hand. "After I left your room, I headed to the elevator. As soon as I stepped through the double doors at the end of the hall, he grabbed me from behind, held a knife to my throat. He dragged me into a storage closet, handcuffed me and gagged me. He left for about five minutes. I figure that's when he got Daniels and the nurse, poor woman."

A cold, sick feeling twisted Rafe's stomach. "He killed a woman?"

"No, no, he didn't hurt her. He grabbed her when

she left the desk to go to the bathroom. Gagged her, tied her up and left her in one of the patient's rooms near the elevator. No one knows for sure what happened to Daniels. Maybe he left his station outside your door to check on the nurse when she didn't return. Or maybe the killer used his disguise as a doctor to lure Daniels down the hall. Regardless, a few minutes after the nurse was tied up, the killer put Daniels in with her. He was unconscious when the killer dragged him into the room. He finished the job, stabbed him, right in front of the nurse."

Rafe replayed Buresh's words in his mind, trying to piece everything together. Something was missing, because the pieces didn't fit. He shook his head. "I don't get the timeline."

Buresh dropped the tubing and gave Rafe his full attention. "What do you mean?"

"When you left my room, Daniels was still outside?"

"Right."

"And the nurse? Was she at the desk?"

Buresh frowned and thought for a moment. "No, I don't think so. I don't remember seeing anyone there when I walked by. Maybe that's when she stepped out to go to the restroom."

"It all had to happen fast," Rafe said, "because there was only about a six minute lag after you left to when the transformer blew. And another couple of minutes before you called my room."

"Right," Buresh said. "The nurse must have been first. Then the killer tied me up, left to get Daniels. He obviously used a timer for the bomb, because the transformer blew while I was in the closet. The killer came back and made me call you. Then he stabbed me, for no reason. I wasn't resisting." He cursed and shook his head. "You did get my SOP reference, right? You got that I was trying to tell you to get out of there?"

"Of course. That was quick thinking, probably saved Darby's life."

"Maybe, maybe not. I imagine you would have figured out something was up pretty soon and would have gotten her out of there anyhow." Buresh waved his hand in the air. "As for the time-line, seems straightforward to me. What's the problem?"

"I called 9-1-1 right after I talked to you," Rafe said. "Immediately after that call, I got Darby out of the room. We were in the hall about five seconds before I heard someone pushing open the double doors. I pulled Darby into one of the patient rooms, and we hid there while a gunman crept through the hallway, searching every room." He tightened his hands against the top of the chair. "I thought he was the bomber, which is why Darby and I ended up in the ceiling to get away. But it wasn't the bomber. It was Jake."

Buresh blinked in confusion. "That doesn't make

sense. How could Jake have gotten up there so fast? You'd just called 9-1-1. And where did the bomber go after stabbing me?"

"Exactly my point. That's the problem with the timeline."

Buresh swore. "Are you trying to imply Jake's the bomber? If that's the case, just show a picture of Jake to Dr. Steele and we can settle this right now." He snorted and shook his head. "You and I both know there are holes all over that theory. He was with me in the warehouse when the bomber kidnapped Dr. Steele. And even if he wasn't, he's a cop. Hell, you grew up together. He's your best friend."

"Was," Rafe said. "*Was* my best friend. Not anymore. You know he blames me for Shelby's death."

"I'm sure that's just grief talking."

"That might explain his actions right after Shelby died. But a year? No, there's something else going on. Regardless, I'm not making any assumptions. And I'm not ruling anyone out. We don't know that Jake *isn't* the bomber. All we know for sure is that he's not the man who kidnapped Darby. The bomber and the kidnapper could be two different people."

Buresh's eyes widened and he started coughing violently. Rafe grabbed the cup of ice chips sitting on the table next to the bed and handed them to his boss.

After swallowing a mouthful of ice, Buresh glared at Rafe. "Detective Jake Young," he said, "is one of us. No way is he involved in this mess. As soon as Dr. Steele is discharged, you get her out of here. I don't want any arguments. You're both banged up and need the rest, so you might as well keep her close so you can protect her. Leave the investigating to someone else. When you're all rested up, get your butt back into the station to work with a sketch artist. And after that, I want you— and Jake—in my office. We'll get to the bottom of this timeline problem. And I guaran-freaking-tee he's not involved."

"You don't really believe you'll be back in the office anytime soon, do you?"

"I may look like hell, and feel like hell, but other than losing some blood, I'm fine. The bomber didn't cut anything vital. Whether the doctors want to let me go tomorrow or not, I'm going." His mouth flattened into a hard line. "I need to be a part of this investigation. I have to look at Daniels's widow and tell her I did everything I could to find her husband's killer."

"Wake up, sleepyhead."

Darby frowned at the deep voice intruding into her sleep. She mumbled a protest and threw her arm over her eyes to block out the bright light that flickered on overhead.

"I let you sleep as long as I could." A hand gently shook her.

She slapped the hand off her shoulder and blinked her eyes open.

When she saw who was bothering her, she groaned and closed her eyes again. Detective Rafe Morgan. She hadn't seen him since waking up from her so-called trance in an examining room in the E.R. He'd insisted on a psychiatric consult, in spite of her embarrassed pleading with him to just let it go. She didn't need another mental health professional to tell her what she already knew.

Dark, tight places terrified her.

"Nap time is over." Rafe shook her shoulder, his touch gentle in spite of the way he'd barked out his order.

Darby let out an exasperated breath and opened her eyes again. The clock on the wall behind him showed her how late, or rather early, it was. "Good grief. It's five in the morning."

"We should have left an hour ago." He plopped a small suitcase on the foot of the bed and pitched a tan plastic bag next to it, one of those disposable bags with the name of a local grocery store written across it.

Realizing her tormentor wasn't going to leave her alone, she sat up, grabbed the plastic bag and looked inside. White cotton slacks, a dark button-up blouse…a bra and panties. Her face flushed hot. "What's this?"

"I had your assistant go to your house and pack you some things. She said the grocery bag has what you need to change here in the hospital. Everything else is in the suitcase. You've got five minutes."

He turned to go, and she realized he'd already changed his clothes. His hospital gown was gone. In its place was a pair of faded jeans and a muscle-hugging forest-green T-shirt. And he was sporting another ominous-looking gun again, holstered against his hip.

"Wait," she called out as he pulled the door open.

He paused and looked at her expectantly.

She pressed the buttons on the bed, raising herself into a sitting position. "What's going on?" She glanced toward the door, her body tensing. "Is… is there someone out there? Is that why we have to leave right now?"

The look on his face softened. He let the door close and strode back to her bed. "You're safe. Plenty of cops this time. But I want you out of here before the sun comes up, just in case the bomber's watching the hospital. I'm betting he might be asleep right now, so this is the best time to go."

Hearing the bomber might be watching the hospital had her pulse leaping in her throat. The selfish part of her wanted to jump up right now and get as far away as she could. But that wasn't right, not when she could tell Rafe wasn't anywhere near recovered from their ordeal in the marsh.

The corners of his eyes were tight with strain, and his face seemed pale beneath his tan. Even though the stubborn man was obviously trying to hide that he was in pain, his head must be throbbing. Because every now and then he winced.

"You have a concussion. You can't leave. You should be lying in bed, being monitored by a doctor. And I'm sure you need some pain medication."

He tilted her chin up. "I can handle a little headache. What I can't handle is you getting hurt. You're far too intelligent not to realize it makes sense to get out of here. Now."

Intelligent or not, all the arguments in her head fled the moment his warm hand touched her. "All right, give me a few minutes."

He nodded and headed out the door.

Determined not to dwell on why Rafe Morgan, of all people, could send shivers of delight shooting through her just by touching her chin, she grabbed the grocery bag and went into the bathroom. After taking care of her needs and using the toiletries Mindy had—bless her heart—included in the bag, she hurriedly changed out of the hospital gown into the slacks and shirt. She was sitting on the edge of the bed, slipping on her shoes when Rafe came back into the room.

"Let's go." He grabbed her suitcase and her hand and towed her toward the door.

That inexplicable tingle of pleasure shot through Darby again. Irritated both with herself for reacting to his touch, and with him for constantly trying to haul her around everywhere, she tugged her hand out of his grasp.

He stopped and looked at her in question.

"I'll walk beside you, or in front of you, but I refuse to be pulled behind you like a toy on a string."

He rolled his eyes but didn't try to take her hand again. He opened the door, spoke to the officer visible through the glass wall and motioned for her to join him.

They hurried down the long hallway toward the brightly lit entrance. He stopped beside one of the two police officers standing near the double sliding glass doors. They spoke in low tones, before Rafe put his hand on the small of Darby's back, guiding her through the doors out to the parking lot. She could feel the tension radiating off him. He continually glanced around. The policemen stood at the doors, watching them, but Darby still felt uneasy.

When they reached the driver's side of a black, four-wheel drive pickup, Rafe tossed her suitcase in the back and pulled a set of keys out of his jeans pocket. He used the clicker to unlock his door and yanked it open.

Darby wasn't sure how she was going to climb

into the massive truck. There was no way her short legs could reach that high. Rafe must have realized the same thing, because he suddenly put his hands around her waist. She let out a surprised squeal when he lifted her up into the driver's seat. It was a bench seat, and she had to quickly scoot over to avoid him sitting on her lap when he climbed inside.

"Seat belt," he ordered, clicking his into place and starting the engine.

Darby shot him an irritated glance because of his latest order, but her efforts were wasted because he didn't bother to look at her. Instead, he kept looking in his mirrors, and studying every car in the parking lot. As soon as her seat belt was on, he pulled out of the parking space.

He started forward, just as a man stepped out from beside another car and stood in the lane about fifty feet ahead of them. He motioned for them to stop. But instead of slowing, Rafe hit the accelerator, making the truck leap forward. The man had to jump out of the way to avoid being run down.

Darby gasped in shock and turned in her seat to look behind them. The man was standing in the middle of the lane again, his hands fisted beside him. Even in the dim parking lot lights, Darby could see the mask of fury on his face.

"Who was that?"

Rafe glanced in his rearview mirror before answering. "That was Jake." He didn't pause at the stop sign onto the main road. The truck's tires squealed as he turned south.

"Who's Jake?"

His hands tightened on the steering wheel. "Jake Young is a detective, and a bomb tech. He's the man with the gun we were hiding from at the hospital. You probably don't remember seeing him in the stairwell since you were basically catatonic at the time."

She rolled her eyes at his "catatonic" comment. "The one who was trying to help us, right? He was searching for the bomber?"

He grunted noncommittally.

"Why didn't you stop back there?"

When he finally looked at her, she sucked in her breath, shocked at the raw pain and bitterness stamped across his face.

"Jake was my wife's brother. He blames me for her death."

Chapter Six

The two double beds in Darby's motel room boasted neon green coverlets with palm fronds and brightly colored parrots. Beach-scene prints decorated the walls. The carpet was a faded royal blue. The room screamed "cheap," but thankfully, when Darby stepped into the tiny bathroom to take a look, it was blessedly clean. Bright white subway tiles reflected the overhead light without a hint of mildew or grime.

She stepped back into the main room. "Which room will you be in?"

The corner of his mouth tilted up. "You thought I was staying in a separate room?"

She folded her arms. "Yes, of course. It's not like we're…you know…courting."

"'Courting'?" His grin widened. "Do people really say that in this century?"

She narrowed her eyes at him.

His smile faded, and in four long strides he was standing in front of her, his usual serious expression firmly in place. "I can't protect you from another room. Like it or not, we're stuck together until the bomber is caught."

The thought of him sleeping in a bed a few feet away had her belly tightening. A memory flashed through her mind...his hard lips molding to hers, his warm hand caressing her bottom as he pulled her close, his body hardening against her. Her breath caught in her throat.

He cocked his head, studying her. "The psychiatrist said you didn't remember what happened when you were in the trance. Is it starting to come back?"

Come back? She'd never forgotten. She'd been frozen, unable to move or respond, but she'd been aware of everything around her. And she hadn't forgotten. She'd just been too embarrassed to admit it.

She remembered *everything*.

He took a step toward her, then another. "In the ceiling, when we heard the gunman below us, you whimpered. I had to kiss you, to silence you. And then I—"

"Stop," she whispered.

He gently lifted her chin. "You *do* remember."

"I don't... I don't want to..." She licked her lips, her gaze falling to his mouth. "I don't want to talk about it."

His hands moved to her shoulders. He braced his legs on each side of her, surrounding her with his heat. "When I...touched you..."

She leaned toward him. "Yes?"

His thumbs traced small patterns on her shoulders, making her shiver with longing.

"I need you to understand," he said, his voice rough, raspy. He cleared his throat. "I was only trying to shock you into moving. You realize that, right? I was trying to protect you. I wasn't..." He rested his forehead against hers.

Darby slid her hands up his chest. "You weren't... what?" she whispered.

He shuddered and took a step back, then another. "I wasn't trying to take advantage. I apologize."

Darby blinked. Rafe stood two feet in front of her, looking chagrined. What had just happened? He'd caressed her shoulders. His voice had thickened when he spoke to her.

Had she imagined that?

Apparently she had. But she certainly hadn't imagined her own reaction. She'd wanted, needed, to touch him, and had desperately wanted him to touch her in return. She twisted her fingers together. She wasn't thinking clearly. Lack of sleep had muddled her mind. She had actually convinced herself that Detective Rafe Morgan, a man who'd never made any pretense at even liking her, was attracted to her—and that she was attracted to him.

How humiliating.

If the floor had opened up beneath her right now she would have gladly jumped in the hole.

No matter how tight and dark it was.

"No problem." She struggled to sound nonchalant. "I understand you were just trying to protect me. And of course it makes sense for you to stay in this room with me. After all, you *are* my baby-sitter."

He frowned and looked as though he wanted to argue, but she grabbed her suitcase and swept past him.

"I'm going to take a shower."

AFTER SPENDING ALL DAY and all night cooped up in the motel room, Darby was more than ready to go somewhere else, anywhere else. Still, the police station wouldn't have been her first choice. But Rafe wanted her to meet with the sketch artist this morning.

The sprawling complex off U.S. 1 that housed the police department was almost a second home for Darby. She'd been in the driver's license office next door a couple of times. She'd been at the courthouse as an expert witness too many times to count. And she was often in the police station to be interviewed by the detectives, including Rafe.

But she'd never been in the police station as a witness to a crime, until today.

The sketch artist sat across from Darby now. Sandy seemed nice enough, but Darby still couldn't relax. The idea of trying to describe a man who'd tried to kill her, and was still out there somewhere, had her clutching her hands in her lap to keep them from shaking. The confidence she normally felt deserted her. "The nose is wrong, but I can't figure out why."

Sandy picked up her eraser and rubbed it across the drawing, leaving a white open area on the page where the nose used to be. "Take all the time you need."

"His nose looked a lot like mine," Rafe said from the doorway. "Except it was slightly crooked at the end, if that helps." He was holding a large, brown paper sack and a cardboard drink carrier with three cups. He set them on the desk. "The guys finally brought subs. Sorry it took so long to get lunch."

Sandy watched him closely, studying his face as her pencil moved across the pad of paper on her lap. She sketched in a new nose on the drawing, then held it up for Darby's inspection. "Better?"

A chill swept through Darby. Until now, the sketch hadn't seemed like a real person's likeness. But now, looking at that familiar face, all the fear and helplessness she'd felt in the boat, the marsh, the hospital, came crashing back.

Her throat was too tight to speak, so she gave a small nod.

A thoughtful look crossed Rafe's face. As if coming to a decision, he pulled one of the sandwiches out of the bag and held it out to Sandy. "Would you mind eating somewhere else? I'd like a few moments alone with Dr. Steele."

"No problem, Detective Morgan. I could use a break anyway." Sandy rose from the chair behind the desk, leaving her pad and pencil. She grabbed her soda and sandwich. "I'll be back in, what, half an hour?"

"That'll work," he said. "Thanks."

"Thanks for lunch." She raised the sub in salute and left the office.

Rafe closed the door behind her, moved one of the sandwiches to the edge of the desk so Darby could reach it and sat down across from her. "I ordered you a diet soda. Forgot to ask what you wanted to drink, but I figured diet was safe. My sisters love the stuff so I took the chance you might, too."

She smiled her thanks and scooted her chair closer so she could use the desk as a table. They ate in silence, and it wasn't until she finished her sub that she realized she'd practically inhaled her food.

Rafe's blue eyes lit with amusement, as if he knew what she was thinking. "Don't be embarrassed. Your manners were impeccable." He laughed when she scowled at him. "You had to be hungry. You haven't eaten since we ordered room service around this time yesterday."

She wiped her mouth and set her napkin down. "What about you?" She waved at his half-eaten sandwich, which he hadn't touched in several minutes. "Aren't you hungry? Are you feeling okay? The concussion—"

"The concussion is not an issue. I don't even have a headache anymore. Besides, I snacked earlier on some vending machine food."

She tossed her sandwich wrapper in the garbage can. "Were you able to find anything out about the investigation? Are there any leads?"

"I'll answer that in a minute. First, you have something important to take care of." He took his cell phone out of his pocket and held it out to her.

"What's this for?" she asked, hesitantly taking the phone.

"With everything happening so fast, I didn't think to offer earlier."

"Offer what?"

"To let you call your family. They have to be worried about you. Even though your name wasn't released to the press, the location of the warehouse bombing was. And your family has to be worried that your office was just across the street, especially since they haven't heard from you." He stood. "Is ten minutes enough time?"

He was halfway to the door when she called out to him. "Wait, I don't... I don't need ten minutes. I don't even need one. But...thanks. Really, I appreciate it."

A look of understanding crossed his face as he

took the phone and sat down again. "Sorry. I didn't realize you didn't have a family. I shouldn't have assumed anything."

"No, I…ah, have a family. I just don't…" She awkwardly cleared her throat. "You said you were going to tell me about the investigation."

He studied her, looking thoughtful.

She tried to sit still without squirming under his scrutiny. Her family situation was complicated, and not something she wanted to discuss, especially with Rafe Morgan.

"Actually," he said, "I want your help on another part of the investigation, aside from the sketch."

Darby let out a relieved breath.

Rafe pulled his chair around the side of the desk next to hers and rested his forearms on his knees. "The fingerprints from the hospital confirm that Daniels and Buresh were both attacked by the same perp."

She frowned. "Did you think there was more than one?"

"We can't make assumptions. That's when mistakes happen. Unfortunately, the fingerprints didn't come up in our local database or in the FBI database. That means our perpetrator hasn't been in the system before. So, we're no closer to knowing who he is. But if we can get a list of suspects together, we'll be able to exclude based on those prints." He shrugged. "It's a start."

"You said you thought I could help. How?"

"You're the common link. The bomber sent the first envelope to you. And then he left an envelope at the scene with your picture in it, when he abducted you."

She blinked at the reminder and tightened her hands on the arms of the chair. "Go on."

He studied her for a moment, as if to decide whether she was going to fall apart or not. "Since he doesn't know where you are," he continued, "we believe he'll move on to another victim soon. When he does, I'd like to be ahead of the game, with a list of potential suspects. That's where you come in. There has to be a connection between you and the bomber. Is there anyone you've had an argument with recently, someone who might think of you as their enemy?"

"Honestly, there are probably a lot of people who think of me as their enemy."

His brows rose.

"Don't look so surprised," she said. "I told you I get a few threats every year. I'm a psychologist, and an expert witness. Both of those roles pit me against plenty of people, from clients' families who don't think I did enough to help their loved ones, to families of victims in court cases where I testified on behalf of the accused. It's a long list. The best thing to do is to get my laptop from my office. All of my active cases are on there. And my backup external drive has older cases. I need my computer anyway, so I can review the appointments that have to be canceled, and arrange referrals for my clients until I can return to work."

Some of his earlier enthusiasm waned. "Just how long a list are we talking about?"

"I've been a practicing psychologist for six years, worked with hundreds of clients."

"Our bomber is angry," Rafe said. "Something happened recently to set him off. I'm assuming the bomber and your kidnapper are the same person for now, so let's limit our search to males only. And let's focus on the past six months. How many cases then?"

"I disagree with your timeline assumption. People can hold grudges for a long time. Sometimes, the anger builds over time rather than diminishes. Especially if someone is mentally unbalanced."

He gave a short, humorless laugh. "I'd say our bomber is definitely unbalanced, or he wouldn't be running around trying to kill people." His jaw tightened. "But of course, that doesn't mean he's legally insane and can get off without doing time for murder once we do catch him."

She sighed and chose to ignore his unsubtle barb, his implication that she might jump on his statement and use it to get the bomber a lighter sentence. "I'm just saying that if you focus on the past six months, you might rule out someone who feels he was wronged much longer ago than that, maybe years. But until now he either didn't have a plan or the means to execute his plan, or something happened recently to trigger his behavior."

He cocked his head, looking thoughtful. "Let's assume we go back twelve months. How many clients are we talking about then?"

She shrugged. "I've personally treated dozens of clients in the past year. Add in the court cases where I've consulted and testified, both here and in neighboring cities like Jacksonville, maybe a hundred. And of course you'd have to consider the family members as potential suspects, too."

He blew out a frustrated breath. "It's better than what I had before, which was absolutely nothing. Let's go find Sandy and finish that sketch. Then you can give me your keys and I'll get that laptop and hard drive from your office."

"You aren't going to my office without me. And you aren't looking at my files without a court order."

"Are you seriously going to force me to subpoena your files? That's a huge waste of time."

"I could lose my license. I have to respect my clients' privacy."

He shook his head, not looking happy. "Fine, I'll have one of the guys get a court order. In the meantime, I'm still going to be the one to go get your files for you—even if I'm not looking at them yet.

There's a guy out there trying to kill you. You aren't going anywhere near your house or your office until we catch him. You can wait here while I go."

"It's not that simple. I'll need my appointment book, my files on other psychologists so I can work on referrals, my notes from recent meetings and therapy sessions that haven't been put into the computer yet. There's no way I'll be able to explain where all of that is, or exactly what to look for."

"What about your receptionist, Mindy?"

"Assistant, not receptionist."

He raised a brow and waited for her answer.

She chewed her bottom lip as she thought about what she would need. "Okay, that will work. I'll ask her to go by my house and get some of my notes in my home office, too. It might take a few hours for her to pull everything together."

He looked at his watch and stood. "We can't stay here much longer. Someone is bound to see my truck and assume you're here with me."

"What do you mean? Our names weren't in the paper. And wouldn't the bomber think I'm still at the hospital? That's why we left while it was still dark yesterday morning."

He gave her a droll look. "How long have you lived in St. Augustine?"

"All my life. Why?"

"Me, too, so we both know how small towns work. The bombing, the boat crash, the search for the gunman in the marsh, Daniels's murder—it's all over the news. By now, someone at the hospital has pieced it together, that you and I were the ones the gunman was after. They've told a friend, who told another friend, and so on. It's only a matter of time until the reporters hear our names and go on the hunt. We need to get out of here, get new transportation and find a new place to stay before some overzealous reporter leads the killer straight to you."

AFTER FINISHING WITH the sketch artist, Darby and Rafe were about to leave the police station when a man stepped in front of the door, blocking their way.

Jake. Again.

"Move," Rafe said. "I don't have time for this."

"Make time. What the hell was that all about at the hospital? You almost ran me down."

"I might ask you the same thing. Why were you hunting for Darby and me with a gun?"

Jake's brows rose. "*Hunting?* I went to the hospital to see you. When the power went out, I figured you might be in trouble. So I went up the back stairs to try to find you. And *protect* you." His face twisted with anger. "Is that what you thought? That I was trying to kill you? Are you really that stupid?"

Rafe narrowed his eyes at his former friend. "Are

you stupid enough to think I'd believe you went to the hospital to *visit* me? Especially after holding your gun on me before those SWAT guys showed up?"

Jake's hands tightened into fists. "Maybe I was being a jerk in the stairwell, but I wouldn't have pulled the trigger. I didn't say I went to the hospital to *visit* you. I said I went to *see* you, to discuss the evidence I collected in the warehouse. To brainstorm about the case that I'm trying to solve." He added a few choice swearwords, letting Rafe know exactly what he thought of his suspicions.

"Uh, Rafe. Everyone's watching us." Darby put her hand on his arm.

Sure enough, everyone in the lobby was watching them. A couple of uniformed officers looked ready to step in, if necessary. Hell, if he and Jake came to blows right now they'd both end up in the tank, meaning Darby would have to rely on someone else for guard duty.

Since he didn't trust anyone but himself to look after her, he forced himself to calm down. He drew a deep breath.

"Get out of my way, Jake."

Jake shook his head. "Believe it or not, I'm actually trying to help. You can't go out this way." He pointed through the glass doors to the parking lot. "The *St. Augustine Record* has a reporter sitting in a silver Ford Taurus parked right beside your flashy truck."

Rafe stepped to the side, shading his eyes against the sun reflecting through the glass. Sure enough, there was someone sitting in a Taurus beside his truck, a Taurus he recognized as belonging to one of the *Record*'s reporters—Robert Ellington.

He gave Jake a terse nod. "Thanks. I was going to swap my 'flashy truck' with someone else's vehicle. I'll just call and have him pick me up here instead."

"Take mine. I'll drive yours." Jake held up a set of keys.

Ignoring the keys, Rafe waited for the sarcastic comment he knew would come next.

Jake's face turned a dull shade of red. "Look, there's no angle here. Yesterday morning I was trying to flag you down to trade cars at the hospital, but you practically ran me over. I just want to make sure Dr. Steele gets out of here safely, without some reporter following her."

Wait for it. Wait for it...

"Besides, you suck at protecting people. You need all the help you can get."

"Keep your keys." He shoved Jake out of the way and pulled Darby through the door after him.

As they neared his truck, he pressed the clicker and unlocked the doors. He hurried to the driver's side, picked Darby up and practically threw her inside, slamming the door closed behind her. Darby's eyes widened when he pulled out a pocketknife and turned back to the car beside them.

The reporter was just getting out of his car when Rafe stabbed one of the rear tires. The reporter ran behind his car, his mouth dropping open like a widemouthed bass.

"Hey, what do you think you're doing? You can't do that."

"I just did, *Bobby*." Rafe couldn't resist baiting the other man, knowing he preferred to be called Robert. He grabbed the man's camera, holding it above the shorter man's head, out of reach. He took out the memory card and the battery, tossing them through the open window into the back floorboard of the Taurus, then throwing the camera onto the passenger seat.

Bobby's face turned bright red. "You won't get away with this, Morgan. I have my rights."

Leaning in through the open window, Rafe took the keys out of the ignition and tossed them into the shrubs a few feet away. "Dr. Steele has the right to be safe. That trumps the first amendment any day. Besides, I'm not stopping you. I'm just delaying you. Bill the station for the tire."

He yanked his truck door open and hopped inside.

Darby glared at him. "Don't you think you over-reacted just a bit?" she accused.

"Nope."

"Why not?"

Memories of the brutal home invasion, the sense-less loss of his wife and the press's intrusion into his private life had his jaw clenching. Ellington had been the worst of all the reporters, splashing the story in the newspaper long after other news out-lets had let the story die a natural death. Ellington was the one who kept digging, looking for a motive.

He was the one who found out about the adultery.

That was the first, and only, time Rafe had ever lost his temper with a civilian. Ellington had spent a week in the hospital. Rafe had spent an entire month on unpaid suspension.

He twisted the key in the ignition and gunned the engine. "Let's just say, he and I have a history."

Chapter Seven

Darby quietly watched Rafe as he drove them down a residential street into the heart of St. Augustine's historic district, a neighborhood of wooden two-story houses shaded by centuries-old live oak trees. He'd told her they were going to exchange his truck for another vehicle, but that's about all he'd said to her since they'd left the police station.

"Want to talk about it?" she asked.

"Talk about what?" He put the blinker on, and slowed to turn down another street, edging around a group of teenagers standing near the end of a driveway.

"The reason you're so angry. It's not good to keep that kind of emotion inside. Talking might help."

He shot her a quick glance. "And you're a good listener, is that it?"

"I have a PhD in listening."

His knuckles whitened against the steering wheel. "I'm well aware of your PhD. I've dealt with it in court dozens of times. For the record, I don't put much stock in that piece of paper."

She reminded herself she was trying to help, and that now wasn't the time to respond with anger. She shouldn't take any of this personally. It took about ten times of her repeating that to herself before she could speak again without gritting her teeth.

"Have you and Jake tried to talk out this animosity between you? I'd be happy to sit with both of you. An independent third party can help defuse—"

Rafe sharply turned the wheel.

Darby grabbed the armrest with both hands as he turned into a driveway and slammed the brakes.

The truck rocked on its springs. Rafe unclicked his seat belt and turned to face her. "Are your parents still alive?"

She stiffened, not at all pleased by the change of subject. "Excuse me?"

"Are they still alive—your mother, your father? Unless you were raised in an orphanage, I assume you have parents."

"No, I wasn't raised in an orphanage," she said, unable to keep the sarcasm out of her voice. "I have parents."

"Still living?"

She clenched her hands in her lap. "Yes. What's this got to do—"

"Sisters? Brothers? One of each, two?"

"Why are you asking about my family?" She glanced at the house in front of them. "I thought we were going to borrow a car, trade your truck with someone. Shouldn't we—"

"Do they live around here? You said you grew up here. Are you sure you don't want my phone so you can give them a call?" He cocked his head to the side. "Oh, wait. Maybe you don't have their number memorized. It's programmed into your cell phone, and you don't have your phone with you. No problem. I can call information, get the number." He slid his phone out of his pocket. "What's your dad's first name? Oh, wait. What about his last name? Is it Steele, or have you been married before, changed your name?"

She sputtered, her mouth opening and closing, but she couldn't seem to put a single coherent thought together.

"I'm waiting." His finger was poised over the phone, a banal smile on his face.

She crossed her arms. "My father's last name is Steele, but I'm not telling you his first name. I'm not discussing my family with you. My family is none of your business."

He arched a brow and lowered his phone. "Really? Why?"

She threw her hands in the air. "Because...it's personal. You and I barely know each other, certainly not well enough to discuss..."

The smug smile on his face made everything click together.

"Is this your way of telling me to mind my own business about you and Jake?" she asked.

"What do you think?"

She rolled her eyes and dropped her arms. "Okay, okay. I'll stop asking about Jake…for now." The man was absolutely infuriating, and she hated that he'd just outmaneuvered her.

"And I'll stop asking about your family. For now." He threw his door open.

"Wait, aren't we supposed to go trade your truck for a different car?"

"Yep. That's why we're here." He winked and hopped out of the truck. Darby blinked in shock as Rafe strode around the hood of the truck to the passenger side. Had he really just winked at her? She wasn't sure what to make of that, but she didn't have time to think about it. Rafe opened her door, lifted her out of the impossibly high-up truck and set her on her feet. He didn't wait for a thank-you. Instead, he hurried up to the house where the front door had just opened to reveal a disheveled blond man.

Darby gritted her teeth in frustration. Hopefully Rafe would trade the truck for a low-to-the-ground car that would better accommodate her height. It was really getting old being picked up all the time as if she were a child.

She hurried to join Rafe. The man in the doorway turned bloodshot eyes on her. His lack of a shirt, along with jeans that were practically falling off his narrow hips because he hadn't bothered to button them, indicated he'd just woken up even though it was well past two in the afternoon.

He didn't look too thrilled to see Rafe, but when he noticed Darby, his mouth curved into a roguish grin. "Well, hello, beautiful. Come on in. I'm Nick. And who might you be?"

"D...Darby. Darby Steele," she stammered, a bit stunned at having a gorgeous, half-naked man flirt with her. Before she could protest, he'd grabbed her hand and hauled her inside.

"Close the door, will you?" he yelled at Rafe as he pulled Darby into the kitchen. "I was just about to make some coffee, darlin'. Want some?"

"Um...I...ah—"

"No, she doesn't. I need a car." Rafe stepped into the kitchen, snatching Darby's hand away from Nick. He pulled out one of the kitchen chairs for her to sit.

She sat, enjoying the view as the Adonis who called himself Nick set about brewing a pot of coffee. He reminded her of Brad Pitt in the movie *Troy.* Shoulder-length blond hair, broad shoulders, golden skin. She rested her chin in her palm and sighed.

Nick grinned, as if he knew what she was thinking. Rafe rolled his eyes.

"What?" she asked innocently.

He tossed his keys on the countertop. "Unlike some people, *Nicholas,* I'm in a bit of a hurry here."

Nick pressed the coffeemaker's on button and turned around, looking completely unconcerned. "If you're in a hurry, *Rafael,* maybe you should have called first."

"I didn't think you'd be lying in bed this late in the day. Some of us work for a living and have been up for hours."

Darby wasn't sure, but she thought she heard a teasing note in Rafe's voice.

Nick sat down across from her. "Please forgive my brother's poor manners. If I knew he needed a car I would have had one gassed up and ready to go. But since he didn't bother to tell me, I don't have a car here. And he knows very well I've been working nights, which is why I'm not dressed for company."

"Your brother?" Darby glanced back and forth between them. Other than their basic build—over six feet tall, broad-shouldered, muscular—there was nothing about them that would make her think they were related. Rafe had dark hair, almost black, and deep blue eyes. Nick was all golden, from his honey-blond hair to his sun-kissed skin, and his eyes were hazel. Darby preferred Rafe's dark good looks over Nick's, but that didn't reduce her enjoyment in viewing Nick in his half-naked state.

Nick gave her a long-suffering look "Yes, he's my brother. I'm cursed with two of them. But God made up for it by giving me three smart, sassy sisters who tease both my brothers mercilessly. I'm the favorite, of course." He reached across the table and took her hand in his. "What about you? Are you cursed with a big family like me?"

"I...um."

"Does your fiancée know how much you still flirt with other women?" Rafe asked.

Nick shot him a dark look. "We're not discussing my on-again, off-again fiancée today."

"Ah, so it's *off* again. When are you going to move on to someone else?"

Darby suddenly realized what Rafe had just done. He'd diverted Nick's attention, turning the conversation away from his questions about her family. She gave him a nod of thanks.

He gave her a subtle nod in return. "Since you don't have a car here," Rafe continued, "we might as well go." He grabbed his keys and held his hand out for Darby.

Nick shoved his arm away. "Give it a rest. I can have a car here in fifteen minutes." He leaned over and grabbed the cordless phone off its base on the wall.

Darby couldn't help but stare at his perfect, golden skin stretched taut across his well-defined abs. He spoke to someone named Kitty, telling her to hurry home with a car, and promising her she'd get to drive his brother's four-wheel-drive truck.

Rafe scowled as Nick hung up the phone. "Whoever Kitty is, she's not driving my truck. I just had it repainted from the last time one of your friends scratched it up."

"I paid for that paint job, so you have nothing to complain about." Nick plopped down in the chair across from Darby again. "Tell me, darlin', why is a beautiful woman like you hanging around my brooding brother? You can do much better than him." He winked, obviously implying he meant himself.

She laughed, but when Rafe frowned at her, she tried to contain her amusement.

"Leave her alone, Romeo," Rafe said. "She's with me. I'm her bodyguard. Someone's trying to kill her."

Nick's smile faded. "Who?"

"The bomber in the paper."

"That was you? The boat crash?"

Rafe nodded. "I left you a voice mail."

"I've been using a burn phone. Haven't checked my voice mail in a while." Nick turned his attention back to Darby. "He never could drive a boat. I, on the other hand, am an expert. Ever been to the Keys? I go there a lot. I could take you around and show you—"

"She doesn't need a DEA guy. She needs a bomb

tech. You wouldn't know a mercury switch from a radio-controlled detonator."

"True." Nick shrugged. "But I have other talents." He grinned, and Darby felt her face grow warm.

"When's your girlfriend getting here?" Rafe asked, his voice sounding aggravated. "If I knew it would take this long I would have switched cars with Lance instead."

Nick stood and leaned against the wall. "Kitty's not my girlfriend. She's DEA. We're working a case. Speaking of work, why couldn't you take one of the loaners from the station? Are they too cheap to give you a car these days? What about the impound lot?"

"I wanted a car with muscle, that no one who knows me would recognize." Rafe didn't look at Nick when he said that.

All signs of amusement faded from Nick's face. "Why are you worried someone might recognize the car you're driving? The only people who'd know those police loaners or your impound inventory are…" His voice trailed off and he looked at Darby as if he wasn't comfortable speaking in front of her anymore.

Taking the hint, she pushed up from the table and grabbed the cordless phone Nick had just used. "If you two don't mind, I'll go in the other room and call my assistant. I need to arrange a meeting with her so she can bring me a few things."

Both men nodded, obviously relieved to have a few moments alone.

She left the kitchen and headed into the adjoining family room, crossing to the far side so she could give the men more privacy.

A small scattering of pictures on a metal and glass bookshelf caught her attention. From the looks of it, Rafe and Nick came from a large family. There were several group photos, featuring Rafe and Nick smiling and posing at what looked to be family get-togethers. Most of the pictures were taken outside—boating, fishing, picnicking at the beach.

Even Rafe was smiling in most of the pictures. One smaller photograph, off to the side, showed him and a leggy, beautiful blonde who almost matched him in height. From the way they were looking at each other, she had no doubt who the woman was—Shelby Morgan, the wife he'd lost over a year ago.

Seeing how happy he'd been in the pictures had Darby wishing she'd had the chance to get to know him before he'd changed. Because of his cold demeanor at the courthouse, she'd always assumed he was suffering from survivor's guilt, because his wife had died and he'd survived. But the more she thought about it, the more she realized she hadn't seen him smile much even before his wife's death. When had he changed from the happy man in these pictures to the man he was today? Two years, longer? If losing his wife hadn't changed him, then what had?

Moving to the sliding glass doors that looked out over a retention pond with a fountain in the middle, she punched Mindy's cell number into the phone. Mindy answered on the first ring.

"Dr. Steele, Darby, is that you?" Her voice sounded frantic, making Darby flinch with guilt. Buresh had called Mindy the day she and Rafe were admitted to the hospital, and Rafe had spoken to her when he'd asked her to pack Darby some clothes, but she now realized she should have called Mindy herself, to reassure her.

"Yes, Mindy, it's me. I'm sorry I haven't called."

"Oh, my gosh. I was so worried. I didn't know what to do. Are you okay? Are you coming back to work? I canceled your appointments through tomorrow, but I wasn't sure—"

"Take a breath. Calm down. Everything is going to be fine, but I can't go back to work just yet."

"Just yet? What does that mean? Is that man still after you? What are you—"

"Mindy, Mindy, please listen for a minute. I promise you I'm fine. The police are being cautious and keeping me in hiding until they get this guy. You did the right thing by canceling my appointments, but I need you to cancel a few more, at least through the end of the week. I'll need all of my files for my current clients. Most of my regulars should be okay missing this week, but there are a few I'd worry about if they miss even one appointment. I need to refer them out to other psychologists. Plus, I need some other files, older ones. Are you writing this down?"

"Oh, shoot. Hang on, I'll get a pen."

Darby stepped back to the bookshelf, unable to resist the lure of looking at more pictures while she waited. Seeing a family that looked so happy, so close, was such a refreshing change from her memories of her own family.

She picked up a picture of Nick and Rafe, both with their arms around the waist of a petite older woman standing between them. Darby had no doubt the woman was their mother. Rafe had her coloring, but Nick had her nose, her sensual mouth and her chin.

The woman reminded her a bit of her own mother, although it had been years since she'd seen her. She sent her mother and father money every month, called them on their birthdays and all the major holidays, but since escaping that miserable world when she'd turned eighteen, she'd never had the desire to return, not even to see her siblings.

A wave of guilt swept through her, but she tamped it down. She'd struggled and clawed her way out of the poverty and neglect that had marred her childhood. There was no reason for her to feel guilty about not wanting to go back. She did what she could, by sending money. She didn't owe her family anything more than that.

"Okay, got a pen and paper." Mindy's voice came over the phone. "Go ahead. What files do you want?"

Darby described the ones she needed, files she wanted to go through to try to figure out who might be after her. She also described what she'd need from her house—files, notes, a few more personal items to get her through a week at most. She couldn't be gone longer than that. She'd worked too hard to build her career to let it fall apart now.

"Where are you?" Mindy asked. "I'm at the office right now. I can have this stuff ready within the hour and meet you."

"That fast? Great. I hadn't thought about where to meet. I don't even know the address I'm at right now, but I don't think we'll be here long anyway."

She tapped her nails against the phone and tried to think of a location that was nearby, easy to get to. "All right. I know where we can meet."

NICK AND RAFE FACED each other in the galley-style kitchen, each of them leaning back against a counter, their arms crossed.

"You think a *cop* is involved in this," Nick said.

"Otherwise you would have taken one of the cars from the station. Why do you suspect a cop?"

Rafe blew out a long breath. "I have little to go on and it's too early to make conclusions. It's just that…" He pursed his lips, thinking back to the stair landing, when Jake had pointed a gun at him.

Knowing what Nick would say if he admitted what he was thinking, Rafe debated telling him. But it wasn't as though he could keep anything from his brother. Rafe was the oldest, with Nick eleven months behind, and four years separating Nick from the next sibling in age, Lance. That four years of separation meant Nick and Rafe grew up close, the two of them against the world from the time they could walk. He'd never been able to lie to Nick and get away with it.

"I don't want Jake to know what I'm driving, or where we are."

Nick swore and shook his head. "No way is Jake involved."

"You sure about that? He was searching the hospital rooms for Darby and me, with his gun drawn. He never announced he was a cop, or called out to us. When he found us, he pointed his gun at me." He shook his head. "I really don't know what was going through his mind. I thought he was going to shoot."

"But he didn't."

"Because the SWAT team came up the stairs."

Nick swore again. "Did you ask Jake why he pointed the gun?"

"He said he was just being an ass."

"Well, nothing new there," Nick mumbled. "Seriously, man. You need help. Both of you need help. I know things are rocky between you two, but Jake would never hurt you. He's family."

"Not anymore."

"Family is *always* family, no matter what. Have you ever stopped to consider that Jake isn't the one with the problem? It's been a year since you lost Shelby."

Rafe winced, but Nick plowed ahead anyway.

"You have to let it go, move on. Why don't you just tell Jake the truth? If he knew, it might make it easier for him to—"

"It wouldn't make it easier. Trust me on that."

"Jake's a reasonable guy. At least talk it out. You've been friends since grade school. You can't just throw it all—"

"Don't. Just don't."

Nick looked as if he was about to argue, but the doorbell rang, probably Kitty with the car.

Rafe shoved away from the counter. He tossed his truck keys to his brother. "Thanks for the loaner. I'll get it back to you in a few days."

He started toward the family room, but Nick grabbed his shoulder and turned him around.

Expecting another lecture, Rafe crossed his arms and waited.

Nick shook his head, clearly exasperated. "All right. I'll let it go, for now. Forget about Jake. Forget about everything except keeping your witness safe, and keeping yourself safe. I'm going back to the Keys, back undercover. But if you need me, if you need anything, call. I'll give you my burn phone number. I mean it. I'll hop on the next plane and be here in a few hours, no matter what."

The two brothers slapped each other on the back in what their sisters would mockingly call a manhug.

The sound of feminine voices echoed in the foyer.

Nick grinned. "Sounds like Darby and Kitty are getting acquainted. Kitty's almost as hot as your Darby. Come on, I'll introduce you."

"THERE SHE IS." Darby pointed out Mindy's royal-blue Corolla, parked at the edge of the Aqua East Surf Shop parking lot, just off A1A.

Rafe parked the silver Dodge Charger alongside Mindy's car, but he made Darby wait in the Charger while he got into the Corolla to talk to Mindy.

Darby hated waiting, worried Rafe might intimidate her young assistant, who was easily agitated and too prone to worrying. In spite of Darby's arguments, Rafe had insisted on speaking privately to Mindy about the suspicious package that had started this nightmare. He thought Mindy would speak more freely without her boss around. He was probably right. Mindy probably felt guilty about not being more careful about the package, since it obviously didn't come through the mail. She might not want to admit the truth in front of Darby.

As an administrative assistant, Mindy wasn't the best choice—not at first anyway. She'd certainly proven her abilities later. But when Darby had interviewed her for the job, Mindy had been preoccupied, unable to answer some basic questions, and really didn't have the experience Darby had hoped for. But she was a recently divorced single mom with three kids to feed. Darby had given her the job and paid her an outrageous salary. The price had been worth it to see Mindy regain her self-respect, and to know that her children wouldn't go hungry.

After Rafe got out of Mindy's car and transferred Darby's things to the Charger, he grudgingly allowed Darby to sit with Mindy while he stood guard, his gaze darting around the parking lot as if he fully expected trouble.

Darby tried not to dwell on the reasons for his vigilance. She reached across the middle console and gave Mindy a fierce hug. "Don't worry about work. Stay at home with your kids, take a vacation, on me. Take the money out of the office account."

Mindy's eyes widened in surprise. "A vacation?

I can't do that, not when your life is in danger. Oh, my gosh, Darby. When the police called me from the hospital…and later, when I read the paper—the boat crash…" She shuddered. "I couldn't believe it. Are you really okay?" She sat back, her gaze sweeping up and down Darby. "Detective Morgan said you were stabbed!"

She shook her head and forced a smile. "It was just a scratch. I'm fine, really."

Rafe knocked on the driver's side window and motioned for Darby to get out.

She hugged Mindy again. "I've got to go. Remember, cancel those appointments. I'll take care of the referrals. Then go on a vacation. And stop worrying."

"I'll try." Mindy wiped a tear from under her eye. "Thanks."

Darby got out of the car and hurried over to Rafe. He held the passenger door open for her.

Mindy cranked her window down, apparently not yet ready to say goodbye. "I almost forgot." She held out a lime-green beach bag with bright pink and blue hibiscus flowers stamped on the rattan. She handed it to Rafe through the window and he handed it to Darby.

"You left your purse at the office," Mindy explained, "when you…well, when you went across the street to the warehouse. Anyway, your purse is in there, and the mail from your house and the office. Plus, your datebook. I think that's the last of what you wanted."

Darby set the bag on the floorboard between her feet. "You take care of yourself. Give those beautiful babies of yours a kiss for me. I'll see you soon."

As Rafe drove her away, and Darby watched Mindy's face fade in the distance, she couldn't seem to shake the feeling of doom that settled over her.

Chapter Eight

Rafe drove past the turnoff to the motel where they'd stayed last night, and continued south on A1A.

"Where are we going now?" Darby reached into the beach bag Mindy had given her and pulled out her cell phone.

"We'll find another motel, keep moving every day to a new location until the bomber is caught." He glanced at her. "What are you doing?"

"Checking my cell phone battery. It's low. I'll have to charge it." She reached down to see if Mindy had put a car charger in the bag.

"Turn it off. Now." His deep voice cut through her musings.

She paused. "Why?"

"Because your phone can be traced."

"You think the bomber is savvy enough to know my cell phone number, and to be able to trace it?"

"He's sophisticated enough to create a bomb with a timer accurate enough to match a second timer he sends to the people he wants to torment, right down to the second. So, yeah, I think he could trace your cell phone."

That feeling of doom settled over her again. She powered the phone off and dropped it to the bottom of the bag.

"What about *your* cell phone? Can he trace that, too?"

"I'm carrying a burn phone. Prepaid, no contract, which basically means untraceable."

Desperate to do something mundane, something *normal,* she grabbed the stack of mail from the beach bag. Thumbing through it, she could already tell it was full of the usual—bills, correspondences from lawyers, a letter from her mom and a card—probably an invitation to her mom's birthday party next week. Mom invited her every year, even though she knew Darby wouldn't show. She dropped the mail back into the beach bag, and froze.

Another envelope wasn't bundled with the rest, probably because it was too big. She started to shake as she stared down into the bag. The envelope was white, not manila. And it had a postmark.

But the handwriting was the same familiar scrawl she'd seen before.

"Rafe." She'd tried to shout, but her voice came out in a cracked whisper.

"Don't touch it." He was already pulling over, the car's wheels crunching on the narrow strip of crushed shells and hard-packed sand beside the highway.

He threw the car in Park and reached behind Darby's seat. He drew his hand back, holding a small, black satchel. He pulled a pair of white latex gloves out of the satchel and tugged them on before easing the envelope from the beach bag.

Darby clutched her hands in her lap as she watched a repeat of when he'd been in her office a few days ago. He used a small penlight to examine the envelope, gently feeling the bump at the bottom, before peeling the flap back.

When Rafe reached inside, Darby was unsurprised that he pulled out a timer. The news couldn't be good because he grimaced when he looked at the digital face. Palming the timer in his left hand, he reached back inside the envelope and pulled out the expected picture.

He let out a vicious curse, pitched the timer in the middle console and let the envelope and picture drop to his lap. The tires sent up a cloud of crushed shells and sand as he stomped the accelerator, turning around and racing back in the direction they'd just come from.

He punched some buttons on his phone, then barked a series of instructions and an address.

Darby's insides went hot and cold when she heard the location. She grabbed the photograph.

Oh, please, no.

Mindy.

THE BOMBER HAD TAKEN the photograph from a distance, across the street from Darby's office building, probably from the same warehouse where he'd killed the A.D.A. In the picture, Mindy was sitting in her car in the office parking lot, smiling, waving—probably at Darby—just as she did every day when she and Darby were leaving work, following their normal routine.

Nothing was routine anymore.

Rafe whipped through traffic back to the surf shop. Darby prayed harder than she'd ever prayed in her life.

Please let her be okay. Let Mindy be okay.

But she already knew, even before Rafe barreled back into the parking lot, what they would find. Or rather, what they *wouldn't* find.

Because Mindy wasn't answering her phone.

Ignoring Rafe's earlier demand that she keep her cell phone off, Darby had frantically called Mindy over and over on the short ride back, while Rafe used his phone to talk to the police.

Two patrol cars, lights flashing, whirled into the lot just as Rafe screeched to a stop.

"Stay inside the car." Rafe grabbed the timer

from the middle console. He dropped it into his shirt pocket, and hopped out of the car to meet with the officers.

Darby hadn't even looked at the timer. She'd forgotten about it in her desperate bid to reach Mindy on the phone.

How much time did Mindy have?

When Rafe slid back into the driver's seat, the police cars took off in opposite directions. One of them peeled out, heading north on State Road 312 back toward town. The other headed south, where A1A looped around to Beach Road. Rafe hit the gas, his tires squealing as he turned right onto Anastasia Boulevard.

"How much time does she have?" Darby asked, clutching the armrest when Rafe swerved around a slow-moving car.

"Forget about the timer. Look for Mindy's Corolla. You look right. I'll look left."

He cursed and swerved to avoid another slow car, which pretty much encompassed most of the traffic. The speed limit was barely above walking-speed in this heavy beach-goer, tourist area. Without the benefit of police lights or a siren, Rafe had to be creative about getting around the other cars without running into anyone.

Darby swallowed hard against the lump in her throat. "What if he didn't take her car? What if she was driving her car and he forced her off the road or something? And then took off with her in another car?"

He didn't look surprised by her question, which told her he'd already considered that possibility. "The Corolla is our only lead right now. Best case, he didn't grab her yet and we find her in her car, unharmed."

Darby's chin quivered and she fought against the urge to cry. "What's the worst case?"

His jaw tightened. "Worst case, exactly what you said. He followed her, forced her off the road and took her in another car. A detective back at the station is already working with the managers of the surf shop and the fast-food restaurant next to it to pull surveillance footage. Another officer will head to the scene to interview witnesses, see if anyone saw anything. In the meantime, there's a BOLO on the Corolla."

"BOLO?"

"Be on the lookout. Basically, every cop in St. Johns County is on the alert for her car, including the state troopers headquartered off State Road 16. That's a lot of manpower." He squeezed her fingers where they lay on top of her thigh. "We'll find her."

She nodded, staring out the window, looking down every little street they passed, studying every strip mall. Yes, they'd find her.

But would they find her in time?

The car swerved, throwing her against Rafe. Cars honked as he turned down a small two-lane road.

"That might be her." He grabbed his cell phone and called the station. He barked at dispatch, telling them his location and that he'd spotted a "possible" on the car in the BOLO.

He zipped past a sign declaring they were entering Anastasia State Park.

Darby squinted and shaded her eyes against the sun, trying to see what he'd seen. But the long line of cars in front of them was slowing for the guard shack, each one waiting their turn to pay the entry fee. "Where's her car? I don't see it."

He honked his horn and swerved back to his side of the road to avoid an oncoming car. "There." He pointed to the guard shack. A blue Corolla had just paid the toll and accelerated away at a quick rate of speed.

"Are you sure that's Mindy's car?" The license plate was too far away for her to read.

"No, but I'll know in a minute." He stomped the accelerator and the Charger leaped forward, reminding her that he'd told his brother he wanted a car with muscle. He whipped around the guard shack, sliding on the slick, crushed-shell shoulder of the road before the tires caught and spit the car back onto the asphalt.

The Corolla was fifty yards ahead. It had slowed

for another car, but zipped around it and disappeared around a curve in the narrow road.

"That's her car," Rafe said. "The numbers on the plate match." He raced toward the curve then slammed his brakes, narrowly missing the bumper of a camper that pulled out in front of them.

He tried to pass but had to swerve back into his lane to avoid hitting a pickup head-on. He honked the horn, but the camper slowed instead of speeding up, probably thinking he was just a rude driver and they were trying to teach him some manners.

By the time Rafe got around the camper, there was no sign of the Corolla.

He slowed when they approached a turnoff to a side road.

"What do we do now?" Fear for Mindy had Darby twisting her hands together.

"This main drag is the only way in or out of the park. If I turn down one of these side roads, I could lose him if he comes back out a different side road."

"We can't just sit here, not when he's got Mindy."

His lips thinned as he pulled to the shoulder. "That's exactly what we have to do. We don't have a choice. We sit here until the park is sealed off." He grabbed his phone again and called the police station, speaking in some kind of cop codes she didn't understand.

Darby tried not to think about what could be happening to Mindy. She glanced at Rafe, then suddenly lunged over and swiped the timer out of his shirt pocket. He grabbed it back from her, but not before she saw the digital readout—00:19:04.

Nineteen minutes, four seconds.

Oh, Mindy, no.

She flung her door open and hopped out of the car.

"Darby, wait! Get back here."

She turned around in the road to face him. He was leaning out the driver's side window, his cell phone at his ear, motioning for her to get back in the car.

"Nineteen minutes," she yelled. "He's not taking her out of the park, not if he plans to kill her in nineteen minutes. The bomb is here somewhere."

He got out of the car and shoved his phone into the pocket of his jeans. "Don't you think I know that?" His face mirrored his exasperation when he reached her.

She stared at him in confusion. "If you know that, then why aren't we looking for her?"

The sound of engines running and tires crunching had her turning to see a long line of cars pouring out of one of the side roads at a fast clip. A park ranger, riding a bicycle, emerged from the same side road, waving the cars forward.

Rafe pulled Darby to the side of the road.

"You're evacuating the park," she accused. "Instead of looking for Mindy!"

"Backup will be here soon. Until then, the rangers are at the entrance, checking every car for her. But, yes, the goal is to get everyone out of the park as quickly as possible."

"What about Mindy? What are you doing to get *her* out?"

"There's nothing we can do for her right now. The park is full of families, children and possibly a bomb. The bomb squad is on the way, but chances are the bomb will blow before they get here. We have to get these people out. And you need to wait in the car while I help with the evacuation, just until backup arrives." He grabbed her arm and hauled her to the car. He shoved her back into the passenger seat, clipped his badge on his shirt and ran to meet the park ranger.

From what Darby could hear of their conversation, the ranger had gotten a call over his radio about the bomber and had started the evacuation of the people who'd been parked down the side road to their right. But there were other camping areas within the park, and not enough park rangers to warn everyone.

Rafe told him to go spread the word, get the other campers evacuating. The ranger took off on his bike, while Rafe stepped to the road, directing traffic to use both the east and westbound lanes to exit. He waved his arms in a rapid circle, encouraging them to move faster. Soon they were zooming by, back toward the entrance.

Understanding *why* Rafe was abandoning Mindy didn't make it hurt any less. Darby had been where Mindy was before. She'd been the one who'd been abandoned. She'd been the one fighting for her life, when she'd fallen down a well at the age of seven.

For three days she'd screamed for help until her throat was raw, but help had never come. Her family—her mother, her father, her sisters and brothers—had never come looking for her. She'd gotten herself out of that well, and had learned a powerful lesson. Never trust or rely on anyone but yourself.

And don't wait for help that will never come.

"*You* may have decided to abandon Mindy," she said, watching Rafe through the windshield, "but I never will."

She eased the door open and slipped out of the car, leaving the door ajar.

She backed away, moving as quietly as she could, slowly at first, so he wouldn't hear her shoes crunching on the shells beside the road. When she was far enough away that any noise she made wouldn't matter, she started running.

Chapter Nine

The sound of shells crunching beneath someone's feet had Rafe glancing over his shoulder, ready to lecture Darby for getting out of the car. Instead, he caught a glimpse of her bright pink blouse as she disappeared around the curve in the road.

"Darby! Get back here!" Every muscle in his body tensed. He took a step after her, then another. Without his direction, traffic slowed to a stop. Drivers tried to cut in on each other. Horns honked. A little girl with blond curly ringlets stared at Rafe through the window of a van that was no longer moving, no longer carrying her to safety.

Rafe's heart slammed in his chest so hard it physically hurt. It was agony not to go after Darby, agony to turn his back on her. But he couldn't ignore these people. He couldn't put one person's safety over the lives of everyone else in the park.

No matter how much he wanted to.

He ground his teeth together and banged his fist on the roof of a car to get the driver's attention. It took a full minute, sixty precious seconds, to get the cars moving smoothly again.

He yanked his phone out of his pocket and called dispatch. "This is Detective Morgan again. Is anyone available yet to direct traffic? And where the hell is the bomb squad I asked for?"

A few moments later, lights flashed from the direction of the park entrance. A state trooper's car raced down the shoulder. He pulled to a skidding stop just inches behind the Charger, got out and raced over to Rafe.

"I've got this, sir." The trooper stepped into the lanes of traffic and began to unsnarl the bottleneck that had started as soon as rubberneckers had seen the flashing lights on his car.

Rafe clapped him on the shoulder. "Thanks, man." He ran to his car and hopped in. The powerful car fishtailed onto the edge of the road, almost hitting another car. Rafe swore and let up on the gas. He took off at a slower pace this time, driving down the shoulder, even though it nearly killed him to go so slow.

When he rounded the curve where Darby had disappeared, there was no sign of her. There was no sign of anyone. This part of the park was deserted.

He steered the car back onto the road and rolled down his window, searching each turnoff as he crept forward, looking for the flash of her bright pink top.

There, up ahead, was the parking lot adjacent to the beach, right by the dunes.

And in the middle of the lot was a dark blue Corolla.

RAFE GRABBED HIS PHONE and reported what he'd found. He pulled his car to a stop beside Mindy's abandoned car and jumped out. "What's the ETA on the bomb squad?" he barked into the phone.

"Six minutes."

He didn't have six minutes.

Rafe had to assume Darby had found the car, too. Was the bomber there when she got here? Had he grabbed her and put her with Mindy? Without knowing what had happened, Rafe had to work with the only clue he had. The Corolla.

He shoved the phone into his pocket and looked through the driver's window. Empty. He dropped to his knees and looked underneath. No obvious trip wires or booby traps, but that didn't mean there weren't any.

He jumped up and ran to the trunk.

"Darby? Mindy?" No answer. What if they were in the trunk, unconscious? In this heat, they wouldn't last long.

He glanced at his watch.

Three minutes until the bomb would explode.

Maybe not even that. The bomber could have set the timer differently on the bomb than on the timer he'd sent in the mail. It wouldn't be the first time a bomb maker tried to fool a bomb tech, take him out along with the bomb.

Sweat trickled between his shoulder blades. He ran back to the driver's side window. His training told him to wait for backup. His training told him to wait for the bomb squad. His training told him not to touch the car.

To hell with his training.

He tried the driver's door. Locked. He kicked the window. Nothing. Another kick, harder. The glass cracked into a spiderweb pattern. A third kick, and the window shattered, raining shards of glass all over the inside of the car and pinging across the asphalt underneath.

Rafe reached in to unlock the door. He yanked it open, grabbed the trunk release on the floor. He held his breath and pulled the lever. A dull thump sounded as the trunk popped open.

He began to breathe again, in short, choppy pants as adrenaline kicked in. He tugged his gun out of his holster and raced toward the back of the car. He crouched low, then swung around the side, aiming his gun into the trunk.

Empty. No bomber in hiding.

No Darby. No Mindy.

Where were they?

He checked his watch again.

Two minutes.

Think, think, think. He drew a deep breath of salty air, trying to clear his mind. If he were the bomber, and parked in this parking lot, what would he do? He turned in circles, looking at his surroundings. If he were the bomber, where would he go?

Not back toward the road. He might run into other people.

Not into the trees. There were campsites all over the park. Too many potential witnesses.

Where then?

In front of him, white, bleached sand dunes jutted up into the skyline. Even though he couldn't see the ocean, he could hear it. Waves crashing, miles of water stretching toward the horizon. No fences, no roads, nothing to stop a man who'd already proven he was comfortable around boats. Maybe the bomber's plan all along had been to escape into the ocean. Maybe he had a boat anchored just past the waves, waiting.

Rafe took off in a sprint. When he reached the edge of the parking lot, he ran down the wooden planked sidewalk that led toward the beach. His shoes made a hollow sound, broadcasting his location.

Every move he was making felt wrong. Everything he was doing *was* wrong. He was breaking standard operating procedure, charging forward without backup, making noise when he should have been going slow and quiet, playing it safe.

He didn't have a choice. He couldn't wait for backup. He couldn't play it safe.

There wasn't enough time.

A high-pitched scream galvanized him forward. He pumped his arms and legs faster, leaving the boardwalk, topping the nearest dune just as another scream sounded out, followed by a name. Mindy. Someone was crying her name.

Darby.

The wind snatched the sound of her screams before he could tell which direction they were coming from. When he reached the top of the next dune, the dark blue ocean spread out before him. A hundred yards away, a man and a woman struggled in the surf. He shoved her head under the water. The flash of the woman's pink top had Rafe's heart wrenching in his chest.

He held his gun out in front of him and sprinted forward. "Police, stop!"

The man didn't seem to notice or hear him over the wind and surf.

Rafe felt as though he was running in place, getting nowhere. The sand kept shifting under his feet, slowing him down. He took aim at the man in the water. Could he get a clear shot without hitting Darby? The man's head turned his way. He yanked

Darby up out of the water and held her in front of him like a shield.

She flailed wildly in his arms, coughing, sputtering, desperately trying to get away. She kept trying to throw herself back into the water.

What was she doing?

"Police, stop!" Rafe yelled again as he followed the direction of Darby's gaze. She was staring at a body. Facedown. Floating in the surf. Mindy.

Darby's desperate screams tore at Rafe's heart.

The bomber held Darby in front of him, his thick arm pressed against her throat, his other hand buried in her hair, yanking her head back.

"Let her go!" Rafe stopped ten feet away. The face of the man from the boat stood staring back at him.

"Drop the gun or I'll crush her windpipe."

"Help Mindy." Darby clawed at the hand against her throat, her eyes pleading with Rafe. "Help Mindy!"

Rafe threw his gun onto the sand, out of reach from the man holding Darby, and away from the water.

The bomber heaved Darby into the ocean and took off running toward the dunes.

Rafe hesitated, not sure whether to go after Darby or the bomber. Darby made the decision for him. She dove into the water, streaking away from him with powerful strokes, completely in her element as she swam toward Mindy.

Rafe ran for his gun, lunging, coming up in a crouch and aiming at the fleeing man. "Stop, or I'll shoot!" The man didn't stop. Rafe squeezed the trigger.

The man cried out and stumbled, clutching his shoulder. He lurched forward, and disappeared over a dune into the twisted sand oaks beyond.

Rafe cursed and threw his gun back on the sand to keep it dry. He tossed his phone beside the gun, then waded into the surf. When he reached Darby, she was trying to give Mindy CPR with the waves buffeting both of them. He plucked Mindy out of the surf and grabbed Darby's hand.

He slogged through the water back to the beach. Dropping to his knees, he laid Mindy flat on her back. He put his ear next to her mouth, listening for breath sounds. Nothing. He pressed his finger to her neck, checking for a pulse. Again, nothing.

He put his hands in the center of her chest and started compressions.

Darby crumpled to the sand across from him, wringing her hands and staring in horror at her friend.

"Where's the bomb?" Rafe asked. He pinched Mindy's nose closed and blew two quick breaths into her lungs before starting chest compressions again. "Darby." His voice was louder this time, to break through her panic. "Did he tell you where he hid the bomb?"

She blinked, staring up at him. Some of the wildness left her eyes. "There is no bomb. He was laughing about the police wasting their time trying to find one, even though there wasn't one."

No bomb.

Relief swept through him. Then he met Darby's gaze. Her eyes were filled with hurt, and something else. Accusation? Hell. She probably blamed him for what had happened to Mindy. She probably thought he'd wasted his time evacuating the park.

"Grab my phone." He motioned with his head toward the dry sand where his phone and gun lay side by side.

Darby scrambled across the sand and grabbed the phone.

"Call 9-1-1 and tell them Officer Morgan needs assistance, and an ambulance. Tell them to proceed with caution, suspect possibly armed, extremely dangerous. Can you do that?"

More chest compressions.

Darby's face was pale and drawn, but she made the call.

Two quick breaths. Rafe didn't think Mindy had a chance, but he couldn't stop CPR, not with Darby watching his every move. Not when her face was so strained, her eyes haunted and miserable.

She looked toward the dunes. When she looked

back at him, she shoved the phone into his shirt pocket. "I'll take care of her. Go, find the man who did this. Go."

She shoved his hands away, pinched Mindy's nose and puffed two deep breaths into her mouth. She sat back and began pumping Mindy's chest, just as proficient at CPR as she was at swimming.

Rafe hesitated, desperately wanting to go after the bomber, but not wanting to leave Darby unprotected. A shout had him looking back up the beach. A uniformed cop topped the sand dune from near the parking lot and started running toward them.

Rafe waved his badge and pointed at Darby. The officer gave him a thumbs-up and ran toward the two women. Rafe grabbed his gun and took off after the bomber.

LARGE RED SPLOTCHES of blood marred the sand's pristine surface, leading Rafe over the dune, into the scrub brush and sand oaks. The trail was harder to follow here, on the hard-packed soil.

He settled in for the hunt, falling back on his training. He didn't want to rush in and end up clocked over the head like after the boat accident. Twenty feet into the scrub, a small snap—like a twig being stepped on—sounded off to his right. He froze and waited. Another snap. There, in the trees fifty yards away, the outline of a man, hunched over. When the man started moving again, Rafe crept through the scrub after him.

He eased behind the same tree where the man he'd seen had paused a few moments earlier. The bomber was twenty feet in front of him, in a clearing. Rafe stepped into the open. "Police. Freeze. Put your hands up!"

The bomber stiffened and whirled around.

A shot rang out. Rafe dove to the sand, rolling until he reached the cover of another tree. He peeked around the trunk to see if he could get a better line on where the bomber was. But the man standing in the clearing wasn't the bomber.

He was Jake Young.

The bomber was lying on the ground at his feet, his eyes closed, a wet, red stain spreading across the sand beneath him.

Jake squatted beside the body. He pressed his fingers against the carotid artery, checking for a pulse.

Rafe stepped out from behind the tree, aiming his gun at his former friend. "Drop the gun, Jake."

Jake cursed and pitched his gun on the dirt. "I was trying to save your life, you ass."

"The only gun I see on the ground is yours."

"That's because the dead guy didn't have a gun." Jake let out a wry, humorless laugh and held up a ring of keys. "This is what he was holding. I saw the flash of metal and thought he was going to shoot you. I can only guess he was making his way back to his car, and that's why he had his keys out. Idiot."

"Funny how you keep showing up wherever the bomber is, supposedly wanting to protect me."

Jake's mouth twisted into a sneer. Whatever he was about to say was cut off when a pale, weak-looking Captain Buresh stepped into the clearing, along with a group of uniformed officers.

Buresh took one look at Rafe and Jake, and his face turned a mottled shade of red. "Holster your weapon, Detective Morgan. Whatever's going on between you two can wait. Right now I want someone to tell me why I have a half-drowned secretary on her way to the hospital, a psychologist yelling about someone needing backup, and a dead suspect who looks like he's been shot in the back." He narrowed his eyes. "Whose gun is on the ground?"

"Mine," Jake said.

"Someone want to tell me why I don't see a gun in the suspect's hand?"

Rafe stepped forward, cutting off whatever Jake was about to say. "The suspect had a metallic object in his hand and turned on me in a threatening manner. Detective Young had no way to clearly see whether the object was a gun or not. He made a split-second decision to save another officer's life. I would have done the same thing, sir."

"Oh, you would have, would you? And I suppose that's why you drew your gun on a fellow officer?"

Rafe gritted his teeth together. "A misunderstanding, sir."

Jake snorted and crossed his arms.

Buresh swore a blue streak. "We'll get to the bottom of this back in my office. But regardless of what happened here, or why, I need your gun, Jake. And your badge, pending an internal investigation into the shooting. And since you took a life, you have to see the shrink. You don't come back until you have a piece of paper from the doctor saying you can come back. You got that?"

Jake's jaw clenched. He unclipped his badge and slapped it into Buresh's palm. He unloaded his gun, and handed that over, too. "I don't need to see a head doctor."

"SOP. No amount of complaining is going to change that. Now go. Both of you. I'll meet you back at the station. I want every single detail about what happened here."

Jake stalked off into the trees.

Chapter Ten

Darby tapped her nails on the desk in the squad room, waiting for Rafe to finish his interview with his boss. After giving her statement, she'd wanted to go straight to the hospital to check on Mindy. But Buresh wanted her to wait in case he thought of more questions for her after talking to Rafe and Jake. Since the poor man had been stabbed by the same person who'd been trying to kill her, she didn't feel she could refuse his request.

"Thanks for not scratching the Charger."

Darby glanced up in surprise to see Rafe's brother Nick standing over her.

"When I heard about the shooting," he continued, "I expected to find a few bullet holes or at least some scratches. But the car is sitting out front, pretty as you please, not a scratch on it. Thanks."

"Um, you're welcome?"

He grinned and plopped down in an unoccupied chair at another desk. He rolled over next to her, stretching his long legs out in front of him and crossing his arms behind his head. Unlike the officers milling around the room or sitting at their desks, casting surreptitious glances toward Buresh's glass-walled office every few minutes, Nick made no attempt to pretend he wasn't watching every second of the tongue-lashing Jake and Rafe were receiving. "How long have they been in there?"

"About fifteen minutes."

"Has Buresh been yelling the entire time?"

"Pretty much. He hasn't given them much of a chance to say anything. I guess it's a pretty big deal to shoot an unarmed man, regardless of what that man did. Rafe mentioned something about the sheriff's office conducting an investigation."

Nick waved his hand in a careless gesture. "That's normal in this kind of situation. St. Augustine P.D. doesn't have their own IA unit. Internal Affairs," he clarified, after apparently seeing the confusion on her face. "They have to bring in someone from the outside to conduct the investigation. From what I heard on the way here, Jake will be exonerated. That's not why Buresh is yelling."

"It's not?"

"Nope. He's trying to patch things up between Rafe and Jake. They used to be really close, which made them his best investigative team. He's wasting his breath. You can't be friends with a guy you blame for your sister's death."

"Why does Jake blame him?"

He slid her a sideways glance, and Darby had the impression he was deciding what to tell her. And whether to tell her the truth.

He looked back at Buresh's office. "Shelby and Jake were adopted. Their adoptive parents died in a car crash right after high school. They didn't have any other family."

"I take it they were close?"

"Very."

"They never found Shelby's killer?"

"Right."

Darby nodded, believing she understood Jake's anger. "Without the killer to blame, Jake is focusing his frustrations on the one who survived. He's rearranged the facts in his head to give himself an excuse for how he feels. He's probably genuinely convinced Rafe did something, or *didn't* do something, that caused his sister to die."

"You think so?" Nick slid her that sideways glance again.

"It's the best hypothesis I can come up with. I don't suppose you could tell me more about what happened? All I know is that someone broke into Rafe's house, apparently a botched robbery, and shot Rafe and his wife."

"I guess since Bobby Ellington splashed it all over the newspapers for weeks, it's really not a secret."

"Is that why Rafe doesn't like Ellington?"

Nick laughed. "Baby, it's not that Rafe doesn't *like* Ellington. He despises the man." His smile faded. "With good reason."

"Let me guess. You're not going to tell me the reason."

"Nope."

She sighed and tapped her nails on the desk again. "What about the shooting? You said you could tell me about that."

"You're a curious little thing, aren't you?" he teased.

"Comes with the job."

He raised a brow in question.

"I'm a therapist, a psychologist."

Nick burst into laughter.

Darby tried not to be offended. "I wasn't making a joke."

He grabbed her hand and pressed a kiss against her fingers before letting go. "My apologies, darlin'. You being a therapist just struck me funny."

Darby had the impression he was remembering an inside joke, but she had no clue what it could be.

He leaned farther back in his chair, and propped his feet—which Darby just realized were encased in a pair of cowboy boots—on the desk.

"What you said is pretty much what happened," he continued. "Rafe got shot in the chest. Cracked a rib, lost a lot of blood, but the bullet passed through without hitting any vital organs. Shelby got hit in the jugular. She couldn't have been saved even if she'd been shot in a hospital. It was a tragedy, all the way around. And I don't care what kind of self-delusion Jake is under. He has no right blaming my brother and making Rafe feel any worse than he already does. Jake is a moron."

Darby blinked in surprise at the anger and conviction in Nick's voice. She wouldn't have expected the half-naked, outrageous flirt she'd met earlier to have such a serious side.

Just as quickly as he'd turned serious, his expression cleared and his mouth curved into that cocky half grin of his. "How about I take you to dinner? Now that all this is over and you don't have to suffer with my far-too-serious brother anymore. You like seafood? We can go to Harry's, get a seat by the window, eat lobster while we watch the boats sail by Castillo de San Marcos. Or we could go to The Columbia off St. George Street. Their roast pork à la Cubana is out-of-this-world good. You like Spanish food?"

A gorgeous man—gorgeous with a capital *G*—had just asked her out.

And Darby wasn't even tempted.

She should have been all fluttery inside and excited. Instead, she was more interested in what was going on in Buresh's office. Rafe was sitting in a chair now, looking down at the floor. Jake's eyes were closed and he looked as though he'd fallen asleep against the wall. Buresh was sitting behind his desk, shaking his head.

"Looks like I'm too late. You're already taken."

She blinked, trying to remember what they were talking about before she'd gotten distracted. "I'm sorry, what?"

Nick grinned. "Never mind. I was just testing a theory, don't really have the time anyway. When you see Rafe again, tell him I have to leave earlier than I'd expected, an undercover op. He can leave the car at my house. Another DEA guy will grab it and check it back in. I've already got something flashier and a whole lot faster for this assignment."

"You mean the car we borrowed isn't yours?" she asked as he rose from his chair.

"Heck no. I was driving it as part of my job. I'm a four-wheel-drive truck kind of guy, like Rafe. Only I'm too smart to ever let him drive *my* truck." He pressed a kiss against her cheek, lingering longer than seemed appropriate. "Take care, darlin'. I'm sure we'll see each other again." He winked and headed toward the exit.

Smiling at his outrageous behavior, Darby rubbed her cheek. When she looked back toward Buresh's office, Rafe was staring at her. His jaw was clenched tight. For a moment, Darby wondered if he was angry at her for some reason. But then he turned back toward Buresh.

RAFE CROSSED HIS ARMS and leaned back in his chair. He shouldn't be surprised that Darby had fallen for Nick's charms. Most women did, nothing new there. What *was* new was that it bothered him, even more than having to sit through Buresh's scolding.

"What's it going to take, guys?" Buresh asked. "What's it going to take to repair this rift between the two of you?" Now that his anger was spent, his face was no longer flushed. It was pale and drawn. He definitely shouldn't have left the hospital so quickly after what he'd been through.

Jake's face mirrored the same guilt Rafe was feeling. Rafe stood and crossed to the desk. "Captain, don't you worry about Jake and me. We don't have to be friends to work together."

"Maybe not." He scrubbed his hands across the stubble on his jaw and let out a long breath. "I give up, for now. I'm going home." He pointed a finger at Jake. "You need to go home, too. Think really hard about what happened today. The sheriff's office will have someone over here first thing in the morning to interview you and start their investigation into the shooting. I want this to go smoothly and fast so you can get back to work. And don't forget to check in with the shrink. Understood?"

Jake gave him a tight nod. "Understood."

"And, you," Buresh said, swiveling in his chair to point at Rafe. "I want a full report sitting on my desk when I get here in the morning, including an

ID on the dead guy, with a complete background. I want to know why he chose those particular victims, and how he chose them. I want this bomber case wrapped tight and done with so we can get this place back to normal." He glanced past Rafe, looking through the glass into the squad room. "And escort Dr. Steele home, or to the hospital to see her friend, wherever she wants to go. I'm too tired to ask her more questions right now."

Buresh stood and grabbed the suit jacket off the back of his chair. His hands shook as he shrugged it on.

"If you want to take a few more days, I can cover things here," Rafe said.

Jake glanced at him, a look of resentment on his face. He was normally the captain's go-to guy when the captain was out of the office. But it wasn't as if Jake could fill in when he was on administrative leave.

"We'll see how I feel in the morning," Buresh said. "I might have you drop that report off at my house if I don't make it in. I'll let you know." He sighed heavily. "I've got to work with Officer Daniels's widow to plan the funeral."

Daniels, the officer who'd been killed at the hospital. This would be the first funeral Rafe had attended since… He shied away from that thought.

Jake followed close on Buresh's heels out of the office, not giving Rafe a chance to talk to him.

Rafe let out a frustrated breath and strode toward the desk where Darby was sitting. Her green eyes shined out of her pale face, reminding him again of a porcelain doll. And yet, she'd fought like a pit bull to save her friend today. Rafe might not care for the kind of work she did, but he had to grudgingly admit she'd surprised and impressed him. She could have sat in the car and been perfectly safe while he helped with the evacuation. Instead, she'd risked her life, all to help a friend. And then she'd ordered the cops to go help him, to provide backup as he searched for the bomber.

She stood as he neared the desk, her purse on her shoulder as if she was ready to go. "Detective Morgan—"

"After what we've been through, I think you can keep calling me Rafe. Don't you?"

Her face flushed an adorable shade of pink. She blushed more than any woman he'd ever met.

"Um, yes, of course. Rafe. I thought, because we were in the station, that I should still call you Det—"

"What were you going to say?"

She tightened her hand around her purse strap. "Is there anything else you need from me? Now that the bomber is…well, now that I'm not in danger? I'd really like to go see Mindy."

He hated the idea of her being alone when she found out how her friend was doing. He hadn't heard any updates, but he couldn't imagine the prognosis was good. "As long as you don't mind coming back in for an interview if we have more questions, you're free to go. I can drop you off at the hospital and have an officer bring your car up there so you'll have a way home."

Some of the tension seemed to drain out of her. "That would be great. Thank you."

He led her through the squad room to the parking lot. "I saw my brother talking to you earlier." He held open the Charger's passenger door.

"Oh, I forgot. He wanted me to tell you he had to leave earlier than expected, some kind of undercover assignment."

He nodded, disappointed Nick hadn't stuck around to talk to him. But he understood Nick's job, and that he had his own schedule to keep.

When Rafe slid behind the wheel, Darby turned toward him. "I really appreciate everything you did for me. You saved my life, several times. I don't know how to thank someone for that. All I can say is, if you ever…well, I know you don't seem to like psychologists much. But I'm a good one. More than good. I'm one of the best in North Florida. That's why I testify in so many cases." She smoothed her nails across her slacks. "Anyway, if you ever want to talk, about Jake, or your wife, or whatever…I'm available. No charge."

He tightened his hands on the wheel. "You seem to think I need *fixing*. I don't. My life is fine, just the way it is. And while I'll admit you've surprised me these past few days, and that you might not be the devil I once thought you were, nothing has really changed. Tomorrow morning, I'll be out on the streets, arresting bad guys. And you'll be right back in the courtroom, doing everything you can to let them go. Don't think that because of everything we went through that we're suddenly friends. We're not, and we never will be."

She blinked at him, her mouth falling slightly open during his little speech. Rafe ruthlessly squelched the feelings of guilt that shot through him. Darby had been trying to help. He knew that, but even if he believed in her mumbo-jumbo therapy—which he didn't—he would never sit in a room with her and let her try to make him feel better.

Because he didn't deserve it.

Regardless of how broken his marriage had already been before the night of the home invasion, he should have been able to protect her. He knew more than anyone how dangerous the world could be. He shouldn't have let his guard down just because he was at home. If there was a way to rid himself of all this guilt, he wouldn't take it.

Not when his wife was lying in a cold, lonely grave at the edge of town.

RAFE'S DENIAL THAT he needed help had filled Darby with sadness, but her sadness had turned to cold rage when she stepped into Mindy's room in the intensive care unit. Mindy was lying unconscious on the bed, with wires and tubes attached all over her body. A ventilator hissed as it breathed for her, and the doctors weren't sure if she'd ever wake up. The rage that flooded through Darby had no outlet, nowhere to go. Because the man who'd done this to her friend was dead. There was no one to spend her anger on.

She couldn't help but wonder if this was the same rage Jake felt. Or even how Rafe might feel inside—angry, helpless—with no one to blame for his wife's death because the man who'd killed her had never been caught.

After spending an agonizing half hour watching her friend lying motionless in the hospital bed, Darby escaped from the room and headed to the parking lot. The policeman who'd driven her car to the hospital had stopped at the ICU earlier to return her keys. Darby dug those keys out of her purse now, and opened the driver's side door to her black BMW. She was about to get inside, when a footstep sounded behind her.

She whirled around, clutching her keys to her

chest. She scanned the parking lot. No one. Had she imagined that sound? She quickly got into her car and locked the door. Her mind was playing tricks on her. That's all. There was no reason to be worried. The man who'd tried to kill her was dead. He couldn't hurt her anymore.

So why did she still feel so uneasy?

Chapter Eleven

Darby stepped inside the cool interior of the figurine shop, grateful for the relief from the heat outside. The bell above the scarred wooden door tinkled a welcome, reminding Darby of the ringtone on her phone, the phone she'd purposely left at home this morning before heading to St. George Street, the only "street" in St. Augustine reserved for pedestrians.

After spending the past two days sitting with Mindy's family, watching the hope fade on their faces, she desperately needed to stop thinking, stop hurting. She needed a reminder that there was something still beautiful and good in the world, which was why she was wandering through the shops on one of the oldest streets in the country, unhooked and unplugged from the cruel world she'd been immersed in this past week.

And desperately trying *not* to think about Rafe Morgan.

"Morning, let me know if you need help finding anything."

Darby leaned around one of the glass cases to see who'd spoken. A short, older woman with thick glasses waved at her from the back corner of the store. The feather duster in her other hand never stopped moving.

"Just browsing, not wanting anything in particular." Darby returned the woman's wave.

What she *wanted* wasn't something she'd find in this store, or any store. What she wanted was a feeling of normalcy, to return to the way things used to be. But that was impossible when every time she went to bed she thought about Rafe Morgan—the way his dark eyes seemed to look into her soul, the way his deep voice cut across a room, the way he'd kissed her at the hospital.

The way he'd *left* her, after telling her they could never be friends.

Wanting a man who didn't want her was beyond pathetic. Tomorrow she'd go back to work, reclaim her life. A temp agency was sending an assistant to help her. She refused to hire someone permanent. That would be like admitting Mindy would never return.

She shied away from that thought and the pain that shot straight to her heart. A crystal lighthouse caught her eye. The tiny black-and-red stripes were hand painted to resemble the St. Augustine Lighthouse a few miles down the road. Darby held the tiny figurine up to watch it sparkle. She sucked in a breath when she saw a man looking through the window at her.

He jerked back and disappeared into the crowd of tourists walking past the store. With the sunlight shining from behind him, his face had been in shadow. Darby drew a shaky breath, telling herself she was being silly. That man wasn't looking at her. He was looking at the figurines, window-shopping, like dozens of other people walking down the street.

Then why had he jerked back when she spotted him?

A shiver of foreboding snaked up her spine. She set the lighthouse down and rubbed the goose bumps forming on her arms.

"Did you find anything you like, dear?" The shopkeeper approached Darby, her feather duster dangling from her fingertips, a friendly smile on her face. "We have several more lighthouses in the back, if that's what you're interested in."

Darby was tempted to take her up on her offer, but she'd known as soon as she'd stepped into the store that it wasn't her kind of place. It was charming, and the figurines were beautiful, but she wasn't a figurine kind of girl. The only reason she was tempted to stay in the store any longer was because her stomach was still fluttering from her scare—her unreasonable, totally unfounded scare when a tourist had looked through the window.

Ridiculous.

It didn't take a degree in psychology to realize she needed to face her fears to make them go away. She needed to step back outside, rejoin the world and prove to herself that no one was waiting to grab her and hold a knife to her side.

She forced a smile and shook her head. "Your store is lovely, but I'm not really looking for figurines. Thank you for your time."

Disappointment clouded the woman's eyes but she gave Darby a warm smile. "Of course, dear. There are plenty more shops around here. I'm sure you'll find something that suits you."

Darby adjusted her purse strap on her shoulder, and stepped outside.

WITH CAPTAIN BURESH recuperating at home, and Jake on administrative leave, Rafe was stuck in Buresh's office…on a Sunday. All those times he'd been jealous because the captain always chose Jake to fill in when he was out now seemed pathetic. Rafe's desire to have his captain's job someday had died a quick death after spending the past two days catching up on paperwork.

He'd rather defuse a bomb than fill out one more report, or listen to one more complaint from someone about something he couldn't do anything about anyway.

The door to Buresh's office opened and Rafe

looked up, hoping for something, anything, more interesting than filling out forms. His hope withered away when one of the weekend shift officers walked inside with an armload of mail and dropped it onto the corner of the desk.

"Gee, thanks. Just what I need. More work." Rafe frowned. "I didn't think anyone delivered mail on Sundays."

"Most of it's interoffice stuff that just got sorted. There was one item that came by special courier. I guess they couldn't wait until a weekday. Watch out for all those sharp edges. Wouldn't want you to bleed to death from a paper cut." The officer laughed and headed toward the door.

A tingling sensation had the hairs standing up on the back of Rafe's neck. There was no reason to worry, but he was suddenly feeling a sense of déjà vu. "Wait a minute. You said a special courier dropped something off. Which envelope?"

The officer turned, riffled through the stack, then pulled out a large envelope that was bulging at one end.

A sinking feeling slammed through Rafe's gut as he stared at the familiar block lettering.

No, this wasn't possible.

"Something wrong, Detective Morgan? You look like you've seen a ghost."

"Maybe I have." Rafe dug into his suit jacket pocket for one of the pairs of latex gloves he always carried. He tugged them on and gingerly picked up the envelope. It had to have been mailed before the bomber was killed. He looked at the date stamped on the seal from the courier service.

The package was mailed *today*.

Rafe swallowed hard, adrenaline kicking in, tightening his chest.

The officer sat down on the edge of the desk, watching Rafe gently work the end of the envelope open. Rafe peered into the envelope.

No, it couldn't be.

He pulled out the timer.

His pulse roared in his ears. He pushed away from the desk and stood. The chair slammed back against the wall. Rafe shoved his hand in the envelope and pulled out the picture.

"Hey," the officer said, leaning across the desk. "Isn't that—"

"Yes, it is." Rafe grabbed his phone out of his pocket and bolted for the door. "Tell dispatch to issue a code red," he called back over his shoulder. "All hands on deck."

He ran through the outer office, dialing as he went.

SOMEONE BRUSHED AGAINST Darby's arm. She whirled around, her hand clutched to her throat.

The woman who'd touched her stopped in the middle of St. George Street, eyes wide, her face flushing the light pink of embarrassment. "I'm sorry, didn't mean to push you."

She was obviously a tourist, wearing a T-shirt with a picture of Castillo de San Marcos, the Spanish fort a couple of blocks away. She was holding hands with the man beside her, and both of them were staring at Darby as if she'd lost her mind.

Darby forced a smile to her lips. "No problem. Sorry. I'm a little...jumpy today. Um, enjoy your stay in St. Augustine."

The woman's expression mellowed into an eager smile. "Oh, we are. I just love all these little shops. And we took a horse-and-buggy ride yesterday. So much fun." She smiled up at her companion and they took off into the steady throng of people walking up and down the street.

This was crazy. Darby leaned back against the nearest wall and passed a shaky hand over her face. If she didn't get this irrational fear out of her system, she'd be useless at work tomorrow.

A familiar, small wooden sign hanging over the door across the street caught her eye. The Bunnery. She'd been there many times, but even if she hadn't, she would have known it was a bakery the second someone stepped out the door and she smelled the delicious aroma of fresh baked cinnamon rolls.

Sitting down in a quaint little bakery eating homemade cinnamon rolls might be just the thing she needed to calm down and regain her perspective. She glanced both ways on the pedestrian-only street, and told herself she was doing so just to make sure she didn't run into anyone.

She certainly wasn't checking to see if anyone was following her.

JAKE DUCKED INTO the narrow passageway between two buildings when Darby Steele looked his way. That was twice she'd looked right at him, which meant his skills at following people sure needed work. He wasn't ready to let her know he was here, not yet. Their little confrontation was going to be on his terms, on his timetable, not a moment before. He waited a few seconds, then eased around the corner of the building.

When the door of the bakery closed behind Darby, Jake debated his next move. He couldn't exactly march inside in front of all those people. Darby didn't strike him as the docile type. She'd make a scene. He needed to catch her when she was alone.

He moved back into the shadows to wait.

"BREAK IT DOWN." Rafe stepped back from the front door of the house to give the SWAT team room to maneuver. He didn't know what they'd find when they got inside, but he had the bomb squad van out front with a full team geared up just in case.

"You sure about this, Detective?" the SWAT team leader asked. "Buresh wouldn't—"

"Buresh isn't here. I am. Break it down. Now."

The leader shrugged and gave the signal. One swing of the battering ram against the doorknob and the frame gave way. The door sagged open and the team ran inside.

Less than a minute later they came back out. Alone. One of them spoke in low tones to their commander before the team headed back to the truck.

The commander crossed his arms. "Everything looks normal inside, except for the busted door. You ordered this because of a note? That's a lot of wasted resources. And you dragged a lot of guys away from their families on a Sunday for nothing."

"I don't care one bit that it's a weekend, Commander. Keep your men on standby. This isn't over." He raced back to his car. He hit Redial on his phone and floored the accelerator. Just like the last time he'd tried, and the dozen calls before that, the phone rang and rang.

But no one answered.

He hung up and called the station. As soon as dispatch came on the line, he gave them the cell number he'd been calling. "Get me a GPS location on that phone. Then get every officer we have out to that location, including the bomb squad. *Especially* the bomb squad."

THE CINNAMON ROLL Darby had eaten sat like a rock in her stomach. It wasn't The Bunnery's fault. The food was delicious. Anxiety was what was twisting her insides into knots. She stood at The Bunnery's front window, several minutes after finishing her sugary snack, and still couldn't work up the nerve to step outside.

She studied the crowd of people walking by. Searching for…what? A man who'd died several days ago? A man who could never hurt her again, and who shouldn't have this much power over her emotions?

"Darby, is that you?"

Darby turned at the sound of a familiar voice. The petite blonde woman standing in front of her was the owner of The Bunnery, along with her husband. Darby had known them for years, but she so rarely took time off from work anymore that it had been months since she'd seen either of them.

"Hey, Pam." She hugged the other woman, then cast another glance out the window.

Pam followed the direction of her gaze. "Is someone bothering you?"

Darby fisted her hands beside her. She didn't want to seem weak, scared. But she knew that at this moment, she couldn't step out that door. She hated to manipulate her friend, but she didn't want to get into a long conversation, either, and tell her everything that had happened in the past week, or why she was so edgy.

So, instead, she lied.

"An old boyfriend. He's been following me today. I really don't want to face him."

"Do you want George to have a talk with your young man? I guarantee George can put the fear into him and make him leave you alone."

Darby glanced past Pam to the far end of the long, narrow restaurant. George stood several feet above Pam, and was the tallest man in the kitchen, visible through the cut-through. If anyone could put "the fear" into someone, she imagined George could.

"Would you mind terribly if I just sneak out the back door?"

Pam wrapped her arm around Darby's shoulders and pulled her toward the kitchen. "Of course not, honey. You go ahead and grab one of those fresh, hot cinnamon rolls George just pulled out of the oven before you go. And if you change your mind and want George's help, just say the word."

A few minutes later, with another cinnamon roll bagged and tucked into her purse, Darby was out the back door and in a tiny parking lot that serviced several of the shops. She made her way through the line of cars, emerging between two buildings that faced onto the busy road that funneled tourists through the historic part of town.

Castillo de San Marcos squatted on the green off to her left, guarding the mouth of the Matanzas River just as it had hundreds of years ago when the fort had first been built. Darby hadn't been to the fort in years, and suddenly the idea had tremendous appeal. Losing herself in a bit of history was just what she needed to take her mind off *recent* history.

She hurried down the sidewalk, taking advantage of traffic slowing down for a horse and buggy loaded with tourists, so she could cross the busy street.

When she reached the wooden drawbridge over the moat, a wave of people jostled past her, their footsteps making loud, hollow sounds. They made their way inside the fort and Darby followed behind them. But when the others stopped to look at the glass cases of models and read the historical summaries mounted on the walls, Darby passed through to the open grass courtyard that formed the middle of the fort.

Pausing at the edge of the grass-and-gravel courtyard, she looked left and right, deciding which way to go first. To the right was the stone staircase that hugged the wall, ready to take her to the battlements where she could look out at the river. She decided to save that awesome view as her treat when she finished her tour. For now, she'd head to the left and explore the labyrinth of stone-walled cells where prisoners had been kept, and the rooms where the soldiers had been housed.

The first cell she entered was so low she had to duck her head. A feeling of unease swept through her because it was dark and close, but she forced herself not to give in to her fear. The interior was cool, a welcome contrast to the muggy heat outside. And there weren't any tourists here, which was a big plus in her book.

"Finally, we're alone."

Darby whirled around. If she hadn't recognized the voice, she wouldn't have known who the man was, blocking the entrance, because she couldn't see his face. The sun was behind him.

Just like it had been at the figurine shop.

"You've been following me." She tried to keep her fear from her voice. But this was the same man who'd hunted her and Rafe in the hospital. Her instincts told her to run. But that was crazy, right? Jake was a cop. There was no reason not to trust him.

So why was she shaking?

"Yes, I followed you. We need to talk." He took a step toward her.

She glanced at the doorway off to the left. Did it lead outside, or to another cell?

Jake took another step toward her, then another, his face no longer in the shadows.

Darby moved a step closer to the door, keeping to Jake's right.

His eyes narrowed. "Are you afraid of me?"

"Should I be?" She took another step. "You did say you'd followed me. That doesn't strike me as the behavior of someone I *shouldn't* be afraid of."

A buzzing noise sounded.

Jake swore and dug his cell phone out of his pocket. The light on the phone's screen shined in the dark cell. His mouth tightened with displeasure when he saw whoever was calling. "He never gives up."

Darby slid another foot closer to the door.

Jake didn't seem to notice. He pressed a button on the phone, answering the call. "I'm busy. What do you want?"

Two more steps, maybe three, and she'd be out the door. Her entire body trembled as she eased one more step to the side.

Jake wasn't even looking at her anymore. He seemed absorbed in whatever the person on the phone was telling him. "How do you know it wasn't mailed earlier and just now made its way to you?"

Another step.

Then another.

She took off, out the door.

"Darby, wait!" Jake's voice called out behind her.

She ran through the next cell, around the corner.

"Darby, come back!"

Daylight ahead. She ran for the blue patch of light and burst into the courtyard. She was gasping for breath when she half turned to gauge how close Jake was.

Her stomach clenched and she clutched her throat in horror. "Jake, no. Oh, my God. Jake!"

Chapter Twelve

"You've got to give me a better reading than that." Rafe clutched his cell phone against his ear. He stood on the sidewalk watching the crowds of tourists while he waited for a better GPS reading from dispatch. The Bridge of Lions was visible just down the street. Sailboats lazily navigated the water on the other side of the Spanish fort in the historic district. All these tourists, enjoying the summer day, none of them realizing a serial bomber was in their midst.

"That's the best I can do," the voice came through on the phone. "There's some kind of interference. The signal just disappeared."

"How could you lose the signal?" He waved at one of the uniformed officers who was helping with the search and held the phone away from his mouth. "Check the marina. Maybe someone over there saw something." The officer took off running. Rafe held the phone back to his mouth. "What could cause that kind of interference?"

"Lots of things. Buildings are the worst, something with concrete or brick walls."

Rafe eyed the coquina and stone walls of Castillo de San Marcos, a hundred yards in front of him. The walls were several feet thick. He started walking toward the fort. "What about stone?"

"Oh, yeah, that would do it."

He started running. "If you get the signal back, call me." He hung up and shoved the phone into his pocket.

A shrill scream filled the air. Rafe froze, trying to pinpoint where it had come from. Two officers who were close by stopped as well, turning, like him.

The front entrance to the fort suddenly filled with people. They poured out onto the lawn as if a mass evacuation had been ordered. The scream stopped, as though someone had been cut off in midscream. The hairs on Rafe's arms stood on end. He motioned to the two uniformed officers and pointed toward the fort as he took off running again.

When he reached the drawbridge, he grabbed the arm of a man rushing past him. "Why is everyone running out?"

The man's eyes were wide with fear. "Someone got stabbed in there."

"Who?" When the man didn't answer, Rafe

shook him. "Who got stabbed? Is the perpetrator still inside?"

"I don't know. Let me go." He yanked his arm out of Rafe's grasp and took off.

Rafe stood to the side, helpless to stop the flood of people exiting the fort. He waved one of the cops over. "Crowd control. Stop as many of these people as you can and collect them on the green over there. Someone's been stabbed, and one of these people could be the perp." He yanked his gun out of his holster and held it down at his side. "Get the other uniforms over here and secure the area. I'm going in."

He shoved past the last of the people running out of the fort. His stomach sank and he slid to a halt. Darby was running toward him through the courtyard, her shirt soaked in blood.

No, no, no. *Please.* He didn't know what he was praying for. All he knew was he wanted her to be okay.

He shoved his gun in his holster and ran toward her. She met him halfway, her eyes wide and searching.

"You've got to help him, Rafe. Come on." She grabbed his hand and tugged, but he didn't budge.

He grabbed her by the shoulders. "Where are you hurt?"

She twisted out of his arms. "It's not my blood. It's not…" She shuddered and swallowed. "Come *on.*" She grabbed his hand and this time he didn't resist. He let her pull him behind her.

They rounded the stone wall and he drew up short, yanking Darby to a halt. *No, not this.* He swore and pulled her back to the entryway. "Where's the perp?"

"Perp? I don't under—"

"The person who did this. Where is he?"

"I don't know. I never saw him."

"There are some police officers outside. Tell them to get an ambulance, and to get the bomb squad out here."

She nodded and ran through the entryway.

Rafe turned back around and rushed to the opening of the nearest cell. Jake was lying half in the cell and half on the courtyard grass. Rafe crouched beside him. There was so much blood he wasn't even sure where Jake was injured, or if he was even alive.

Jake's eyes fluttered open. "Darby, is she—"

"She's fine. Where are you cut?"

"Abdomen. I heard someone behind me and started to turn around when he knifed me in the gut. All I got was a glimpse of a ball cap pulled low over his face. I couldn't even tell you how tall he was because I was doubled over." He grimaced, and Rafe wasn't sure if it was because Jake was in pain or because he was disgusted that he couldn't identify his attacker.

"I told you on the phone the bomber sent me your picture. Why weren't you on alert? How did you let this happen?"

"It's not like I just stood there and let him do this," Jake snarled.

Rafe took off his shirt and bunched it into a wad. It was hard to tell where to press, and he had to be careful so he wouldn't move the vest strapped over Jake's shoulders. He pressed the cloth against the largest spot of blood he saw. From the way Jake sucked in his breath, Rafe figured he had the right place.

"I thought I'd killed the bomber," Jake said. "Three days ago. I didn't think there was any danger anymore. What the hell is going on?"

Rafe shook his head. "I don't know. But right now, we've got a bigger problem."

Jake's mouth curved in a rueful grin. "Yeah, you got that right."

Rafe held the cloth pressed tightly against Jake's stomach, trying to stanch the flow of blood so he could focus on his next task.

Disabling the bomb strapped to Jake's chest.

The sound of someone running had Rafe turning. His mouth fell open in stunned disbelief.

Darby skidded to a halt beside him.

"Get out of here!" Rafe leaped to his feet and

grabbed her by the shoulders. He turned her around. "Go on, run!"

She shook her head violently back and forth, her hair flying around her face. "No, I'm not leaving." She shoved his hands off her shoulders and dropped to the grass beside Jake. "This is my fault. I'm so sorry."

Rafe knelt down beside her. "Darby—"

Her mouth set in a hard, determined line. "I did exactly what you told me to do. I told those cops outside what had happened. And you know what they did?"

Jake laughed, then started coughing. Bright red blood sprayed out of his mouth, onto the vest.

"Be still, you fool." Rafe pressed his shirt back against the wound.

"They told you," Jake said, his voice barely above a whisper. "They told you to stay back, wait for the bomb squad. After the all clear, then they'll send in the medics, right?"

"Exactly! They're all morons!" Darby reached across Rafe and swatted his hand away from the shirt. "You can't disable a bomb and stop the bleeding at the same time. And since all your sissy cop friends are too scared to help, here I am."

Rafe clenched his teeth together. If he wasn't so frustrated and worried about Darby's safety, he'd be laughing right now. "My fellow sissy-cop bomb techs will be here in a few minutes, just as soon as the truck arrives with equipment."

"Fine. When they get here, I'll leave." Her eyes were overbright with unshed tears. "I'm not abandoning him. This is my fault. I thought Jake was trying to hurt me. I ran. That's the only reason someone was able to surprise him. I'm not abandoning him." Her voice broke on the last word. She bit down on her bottom lip and turned the shirt, pressing the dry side against the wound. "Go on, do whatever you bomb guys do. Save your friend."

"It's not your fault, you know," Jake said, his voice low and weak. "I should have just gone up to you when I saw you on St. George Street instead of following you. I scared you."

"Why *did* you follow me?"

Rafe gave up trying to get her to leave. He took out his pocketknife. It wasn't much, but it was the only tool he had. He palmed it in one hand while he gently felt along the straps of the vest, searching for how it was secured, feeling for trip wires. If he could get the vest off Jake without blowing all three of them up, he could worry about disabling the bomb later.

"I wanted to warn you," Jake said. "About Rafe."

Rafe hesitated. He already knew what Jake would say. This was the part where he normally left whatever room he and Jake were in at the time. Unfortunately, that wasn't an option. Not today.

"What do you mean, warn me?"

"I've seen the way he looks at you."

Darby's startled gaze shot to Rafe.

"The same way he looked at my sister. He sees something he wants, and he takes it. No matter the cost." Jake coughed, frothy bright red blood bubbling from his lips.

Rafe did his best to hold him still. "Shut up. This isn't the time or place—"

"It's exactly the time and place." He grabbed Darby's arm. "He cheated on her. He broke her heart, and then he was a coward, and he let her die. Stay away from him if you don't want to get hurt."

Rafe risked a quick glance up to see the effect of Jake's tired accusations. But whatever Darby was thinking, it didn't show on her face.

She twisted the cloth against the wound. "We need help. He's losing too much blood."

"No one but the bomb squad comes in until the bomb is disabled…or until it explodes," Jake said. "No one wants to be a pink cloud." He grabbed Darby's arm again. "You should go. There's no reason for you to die, too."

"What about Rafe?" she asked. "Aren't you worried about him, too?"

The anger in her voice surprised Rafe.

Jake's lack of a reply didn't.

He twisted his knife against the cheap lock

holding the vest on one side. A loud click sounded. Darby jerked against him.

"It's okay," Rafe reassured her. "That was the lock giving way, but I can't get the other one. It's wired to explode. Help me work his left arm through here and we might be able to pull it over his head." Hopefully without triggering the bomb.

Darby let go of the cloth. Fresh blood welled up. "What about his cut?"

"We don't have a choice. We have to get the vest off now."

He held the bomb in place while she worked the half-open vest over Jake's arm. Jake's face turned a sickly gray and he surrendered to unconsciousness.

As soon as the vest was over Jake's head, Rafe gently lifted it and set it on the ground. He jumped to his feet and tugged Darby up. "Go on, run, get out of here."

"Not unless you come with me."

"I'm right behind you. Go!"

She took off for the exit.

Rafe knelt down and grabbed Jake's arm to lift him onto his shoulders in a dead-man hold. Jake was nearly as tall as him, and just as heavy. Rafe grunted with exertion as he hoisted Jake's body over his shoulder.

He risked a quick glance at the digital timer on the underside of the vest, the timer he'd been careful to conceal from Darby. When he saw the numbers counting down, a sick feeling shot through him.

He stumbled to his feet, but even as he lunged forward, he already knew.

He wasn't going to make it.

DARBY RACED ACROSS the drawbridge toward the large group of police officers standing on the grass outside the fort. When she skidded to a stop in front of them, one of the officers grabbed her arm, steadying her.

"Whoa, there. You're Dr. Steele, right?" he asked, as two more officers surrounded her.

"Yes." She twisted her arm out of his grasp and turned around to watch Rafe and Jake. The drawbridge was clear. Rafe wasn't running across it. Had he already come out and had taken Jake to one of the waiting ambulances parked on the grass?

"You okay, Dr. Steele? Are you hurt?" One of the officers was staring at her shirt.

She glanced down and sucked in a surprised breath at the amount of blood. "It's not my blood. Where's Rafe? I mean, Detective Morgan. He was right behind me."

He exchanged a glance with the other officers. "You're the only one who came out. Detective Morgan is still inside, defusing the bomb." He gestured to some men dressed in heavy-looking, thick dark suits. "The bomb techs are going in now. Why don't you sit—"

An explosion sounded from inside the fort. Everyone dove to the ground. One of the officers dragged Darby down with him, covering her with his body. Everything went silent. No one moved.

Then suddenly everyone was shouting and moving at the same time.

The officer jumped to his feet and helped Darby up.

"Dr. Steele, are you okay?"

She couldn't answer. She was too horrified to speak. Black, angry smoke rose over the top of the stone walls of the fort. And Rafe was nowhere to be seen.

She slumped to the grass, hugging her middle, numbly staring at the fort. She shook off the officer's hands when he tried to help her up again. He mumbled something to one of the other men and they stepped a few feet away, giving her space.

The smoke quickly cleared, and a group of policemen and bomb techs moved as one across the drawbridge. Their faces were drawn and sober, telling Darby what she already knew. They'd just lost one of their own—no, *two*. Rafe and Jake had both been killed.

Hot tears splashed down onto her hands, and it was then that she realized she was crying. She covered her face and gave in to the deep, racking sobs welling up inside her. She should have been weeping for both men, but she knew that was a lie. She was crying for Rafe because she'd just now realized she cared about him. He was the bravest man she'd ever met, risking his life every day to protect people he barely knew.

To protect her.

Damn him for working his way into her heart, for making her care.

Somewhere behind her a radio crackled to life. Someone calling for a gurney. The police must have reached the bodies.

The squeak of wheels rolling across the grass had her opening her eyes. Two EMTs ran across the lawn, then across the drawbridge, rolling a gurney between them. One of them had a red box sitting on top of the gurney and he held on to it as he and the other EMT raced into the fort.

Darby brushed the tears out of her eyes and climbed to her feet. EMTs wouldn't run like that to retrieve a dead body, would they?

Hope uncurled inside her. She rushed forward, but a policeman grabbed her and held her back.

"Sorry, ma'am. You have to wait out here."

"Can you tell me what's going on? Is there a survivor?"

"I'm not sure yet, ma'am, but I need you to back up."

Buresh was suddenly beside her, looking pale

and exhausted, but dressed in a suit and obviously determined to be a part of what was going on. "Dr. Steele, you shouldn't be out here where the bomber could find you." He motioned another officer over. "Officer Watkins will take you back to the station."

A commotion had them all looking toward the fort. The EMTs raced across the drawbridge again with a body strapped to the gurney and a contingent of police officers clearing a path through the crowd.

Darby tried to see who was on the gurney, but there were too many people in the way.

"What are you waiting for, Watkins? Get her out of here," Buresh yelled.

"No," Darby cried. "I need to wait and see—"

"Go on," Buresh interrupted her. "Get out of here. You're just putting more people in danger by hanging around. Go."

Darby stiffened at his words, but this time she didn't resist when Watkins pulled her toward the street.

No MATTER WHERE Darby stood, or where she sat at the police station, she seemed to be in the way. The squad room was in chaos. People ran in and out. Phones rang constantly.

Watkins finally shoved her into Buresh's office with strict instructions not to call anyone and not to leave. Going home wasn't an option. Telling her what was going on apparently wasn't an option, either, because so far no one had told her anything.

She curled into the only comfortable chair in Buresh's tiny office, the leather chair behind his desk, and rested her head on her drawn-up knees. Her nerves were strung so tight she felt ready to snap. Who had been on the gurney? Was it Rafe, or Jake? Whoever it was, was he alive? What had happened after she ran out of the fort? Why hadn't Rafe followed her?

The answer had her heart pounding in her chest.

He hadn't followed her because there hadn't been enough time.

Even as tall and muscular as Rafe was, he couldn't easily run with two hundred pounds of deadweight in his arms. The bomb had blown less than a minute after Darby ran across the drawbridge, too soon for Rafe to make it to safety. So what had happened? Who was on the gurney?

She fisted her hands in frustration and rolled her head back and forth across her knees. The sound of the door opening had her jerking her head up.

Buresh stood in the doorway, his brows raised in surprise. Darby supposed he wasn't used to seeing someone else sitting at his desk. She uncurled her legs and stood, moving out of his way.

She gripped the edge of the desk, facing him. He gingerly lowered himself into his chair, his face lined with pain, reminding her of his injuries. A hundred questions rushed through her, but she held them back, trying to give him the time he obviously needed to pull himself together.

He let out a long breath. "I'm sorry you had to wait. I had to take care of that mess at the fort, then go to the hospital, then make arrangements to put you in protective custody until we find the bastard who did this." Another pained expression crossed his face.

Darby couldn't wait a second longer. "Who was on the gurney? Who went to the hospital?"

His brows drew down and he frowned. "Detective Young. I thought you knew that. Detective Morgan saved his life. Jake is in for a long recovery, but the doctors think he'll make it."

Young was at the hospital. Jake Young.

Not Rafe.

She stumbled to the chair beside Buresh's desk. Air. She needed air. She dropped her head in her hands and struggled just to breathe. Despair unlike anything she'd ever known slammed into her.

Wait, he hadn't said Rafe was dead. Maybe she just hadn't asked the right question. A small spark of hope surged through her. "And did…Detective Morgan go to the hospital, too?"

"No." His voice sounded confused. "There wasn't any reason to take him to the hospital."

Darby nodded miserably, grief welling up inside her again. There'd been no reason to take Rafe to the hospital because he was already gone. "I'm so sorry. So very, very sorry."

"Why are you sorry?" a deep voice called out from the doorway. "None of this is your fault."

Darby's head shot up and she stared in disbelief at Rafe standing just a few feet away. Joy and relief warred inside her, and suddenly she was in his arms. She didn't even remember running to him, but she was standing in front of him, resting her head against his chest with her arms wrapped around his waist.

He stiffened, reminding her how inappropriate her actions were. Embarrassment had her cheeks feeling warm. What had gotten into her? She had no clue. She started to pull away, but he drew her back against him, hugging her just as tightly as she'd been hugging him.

"It's okay," he whispered, his lips close to her ear. He rubbed one hand up and down her back in a comforting gesture. "I'm not going to let anyone hurt you. There's no reason to be afraid."

Afraid. He thought she was afraid. She was, but not for the reasons he thought. She'd been terrified that he'd been killed.

The feel of him, the smell of him, was so intoxicating she stayed in the warm cocoon of his arms. Then the silence around her registered, and she opened her eyes.

Buresh was watching her with a thoughtful look

on his face. And behind him, a sea of faces in the squad room were staring at her, some of them smiling, some of them looking outright hostile.

She forced herself to let go.

Rafe dropped his arms from around her, and it was all she could do not to touch him one more time, to assure herself he really was okay. She took a couple of steps back so she could look him in the eyes.

"What happened? You said you'd follow me out of the fort, but when I turned around, you weren't there." She swallowed hard. "Then there was an explosion. I thought… I thought you…" She shook her head and wrapped her arms around her waist. "What happened?"

Rafe gave her a puzzled look, as if he was trying to figure her out. He glanced at Buresh before answering. "There was a timer on the bomb. I knew there wasn't enough time to get out of the fort before it blew, so I ran into one of the cells. Two-foot-thick stone walls deflected most of the blast."

Darby sat down before her shaking legs could buckle beneath her. "Most of the blast?"

"The walls are old, not reinforced. The ones closest to the bomb buckled beneath the force of the explosion. I had to dig Jake and me out from beneath a pile of rubble, but it could have been a whole lot worse. Jake's main injury was the knife wound, and blood loss."

"What about you?" she asked. "Were you hurt?"

"Cuts and scrapes. Nothing serious." His brows drew down. "Are you sure you're okay? You're shaking."

Darby's face flushed with heat again. Why was she always blushing around him? "I'm a little freaked out by all of this, but I'm fine. I don't understand how this happened. Who is doing all this? Was the bombing today a copycat crime or something?"

"It's too early to know yet." Rafe sat in the chair across from her. "But I'm inclined to believe the guy who tried to kill Mindy was hired by the bomber to kidnap and kill her. That's why there wasn't a bomb. She wasn't a primary target. She was just a way to get to you, to hurt you. The real bomber is still out there, and he's not finished yet. He has a vendetta against a specific list of people. We know you're on the list. And now we know Jake is on the list."

"So are you." Buresh opened his top drawer, took out a photograph and pitched it on his desk. "This is a copy. The original is in evidence. This came from another courier right after you left the station to search for Jake. No timer this time, just the photograph with one word on the back."

"Let me guess," Rafe said, eyeing the picture of himself. "Boom."

Darby curled her fingers around the arms of her chair.

"This sicko is playing a game with all of us," Buresh said. "We need to figure out who else is on his list. But first things first. Both of you are in danger, and you're dangerous to everyone around you. Get out of here. Hide out together until this all blows over."

"What's the plan?" Rafe asked. "I need to be involved in this investigation. You can't bench your best detective with this guy spiraling out of control. Everyone's in danger now, not just me or Darby."

"Take a laptop with you. Dial in remotely and snoop through the case files. You can give us a list of people you want interviewed and we'll do the legwork here. That's the best I can offer. Stop in administration on your way out. Have them set you up with a fake ID, some credit cards, cash, a new burn phone. Leave your old phone here, your badge."

"Aren't you going a bit overboard? I already have a burn phone. And no one's going to search me, looking for my badge."

Buresh glanced at Darby. "Dr. Steele, can you give us a minute, please? Just stand right outside the office where we can see you."

She blinked in surprise, but did what he asked.

Chapter Thirteen

Rafe flicked a glance at Darby, sitting outside Buresh's office. She was only twenty feet away, clearly visible through the glass. She was safe, for now. He knew that, and yet he had to curl his fingers around his chair to remind himself not to jump up, grab her and run. Even though one of the female officers had loaned Darby a clean shirt, he couldn't quit picturing her in her blood-soaked blouse and remembering his own terror thinking the blood was hers.

He dragged his gaze from Darby and looked at Buresh. "All right, tell me. What has you acting so strange? What's going on?"

Buresh absently rubbed his stomach where he'd been stabbed. "This case doesn't pass the smell test. There's something rotten going on."

Rafe stilled. If Buresh had said that before today, before Jake had almost been killed, he'd have expected it, because he'd been suspicious of Jake. But now, Buresh's statement hit him like a fist in his gut, sucking the air from his lungs. His mind started racing, thinking through the possibilities. He looked through the glass wall at the squad room beyond. It had always been home, a safe haven, and suddenly it took on an aura of evil and danger as his mind painted everyone he saw with the broad brush of suspicion. "You think the bomber has inside help."

"I'm not saying that. What I'm saying is that he's using our standard procedures against us. He's fast, too fast, in and out while we're chasing our asses to lock everything up tight. He knows SOP, that we have to look at the big picture first."

"Like sending in the SWAT team to clear the hospital. He knew he'd have plenty of time after blowing the transformer to go after Darby and me, because no matter how many people called 9-1-1, standard operating procedure says to hold back and wait for SWAT to clear the building."

"Right." Buresh nodded. "I'm betting Jake scared the bomber away without even realizing it."

Rafe grunted his response, not willing to give Jake that much credit. "You're going to say he counted on us locking down Anastasia State Park, giving him time to escape while we were occupied with the evacuation. But that wasn't the bomber. That was his lackey."

"His lackey doing exactly what he told him to do."

"Maybe," Rafe allowed. "So at the fort, he counted on, what? The confusion of everyone running out of the fort after he stabbed Jake so he could get away? That's not inside knowledge."

"Sure it was. What did you do as soon as people started running out of the fort?"

"Locked it up tight. I ordered everyone to be held on the green to be interviewed."

Buresh raised a brow, waiting.

Rafe cursed. "And then I saw the bomb, and had Darby report it."

"Right," Buresh continued. "Instead of holding everyone to interview, the directive immediately changed to evacuation again. We got everyone out of there, as quickly as possible, to prevent loss of life. I can tell you by the time I arrived, no one was waiting on that green to be interviewed. Every cop in the vicinity was keeping civilians back, and holding vigil for their fellow cops in harm's way."

"He's using our own procedures against us. That doesn't mean he's a cop."

Buresh nodded. "I agree. And we're too small a police force not to be able to account for everyone's location at a given time. No one has taken vacation in the past few weeks or missed a shift, nothing to account for the dates and times our bomber has been active. But that doesn't mean they aren't feeding the bomber information."

"Come on, you don't really think one of ours would do that."

"Why not? You thought Jake could be working with the bomber."

Rafe crossed his arms. "All right, but Jake's a special case. He has motive. Who else around here hates me enough to want to kill me?"

Buresh laughed. "Probably more people than you think." He held up his hand to stop Rafe's angry response. "Seriously, I'm not saying one of our people is doing anything on purpose. You know how it is. Loose lips sink ships. Some guy talks in his sleep to his girlfriend, or says things he shouldn't. Her brother or some distant cousin just happens to be our guy. So, just in case, we can't risk your location being leaked. Wherever you and Dr. Steele go, I want it on the QT. I don't want *anyone* to see anything to clue them in that you're a cop. And I don't want anyone but me knowing where you are."

Rafe blew out a frustrated breath. "This doesn't feel right. I agree the bomber may know something about police standard procedures, but I'm not sure we should spend time looking for any personal connections between our people and the bomber. That feels like the wrong direction for the investigation."

"Tell you what. You come up with a better angle, call it in. We don't have much to go on right now. I've already got a team researching for ties between the victims. But since all the vics work with law enforcement, directly or indirectly, it's hard to know what ties matter to the case. I'm looking for any leads I can get."

Rafe glanced at Darby, reassuring himself she was still okay. He took his badge, driver's license and everything else that could identify him out of his wallet, and placed them on the desk. "The gun I keep. Got a problem with that?"

"Of course not. Now go, get out of here. Don't forget the laptop. As soon as you're settled, let me know where you are."

Rafe tapped his fist on the desk. "At least tell me you've got an ID on the dead guy we thought was the bomber."

"Actually, yes. We put his picture on TV and someone called in his name. He was a small-time thug. Had a juvie record, breaking and entering, grand theft for taking his unforgiving stepfather's car out for a joyride. But nothing to indicate he was anything but minor league. No military or police background, no kind of formal training in explosives. We didn't get any hits on him in the system when we first ran him because his juvie record was sealed. That explains why the fingerprint from the attack at the hospital didn't yield any results. We had to subpoena a judge for more and they gave us his rap sheet."

"A decoy. A fall guy, and we totally fell for it."

"That about sums it up. We're dealing with a

sophisticated perp here. We can't take anything for granted or assume anything. Be on the alert."

Rafe nodded and headed to the door. He paused with his hand on the knob. "I assume you're going back to the hospital?"

"Of course. I've got a man down. I'm heading over there right after I take care of a few more things. Why?"

"When you see Jake, tell him…" Rafe hesitated. *Tell him I'm glad he survived? That he needs to quit being such an ass and get over himself?* What was the point? Jake would never forgive him, and there was no way for Rafe to fix things between the two of them. "Never mind." He yanked the door open and strode outside to Darby.

Keeping her alive until this mess was over was his primary concern now. That was what he needed to focus on.

He was just about to grab her hand when he remembered she hated being pulled along behind him. "Come on," he said. "We're going to a very fun place. Administration."

She hurried to keep up with him. "Administration? Why?"

He held the door open for her. "So I can show you a magic trick."

"A magic trick?"

"I'm going to make us both disappear."

WHEN RAFE HAD SAID he was going to make her disappear, Darby thought it was a metaphor. But he'd done exactly that.

She stared at herself in the dressing room mirror, her hair cut in a short bob that barely brushed her shoulders, dyed a deep auburn color. Not a look she would have ever chosen for herself. Neither were the clothes she was wearing. Every time she expressed a preference for a particular style or color, Rafe chose something the exact opposite.

When she'd asked him why he bothered to ask her opinion if he wasn't going to listen to her, he'd stared at her as if he thought she'd lost her mind. Then he'd calmly explained that he'd listened very well, that to make her disappear he needed to ensure she looked nothing like she normally did. So, he wanted her to wear clothes she wouldn't normally wear.

She sighed and stepped out of the changing room.

Rafe was waiting for her, looking like an arrogant prince staring at one of his subjects, his head cocked to the side, his freshly cut hair giving him a regal look. "That'll do. Keep that one on. We'll take the rest with us."

An hour later they were sitting in a beachside café south of town, eating cheeseburgers and fries, watching the local news playing on a TV over the bar. Grainy footage from someone's cell phone showed the black smoke rising over the fort earlier today and the pandemonium that had ensued.

"You done?" Rafe asked.

Darby wiped her hands on a napkin. "Done. What's next?"

"We're going back into town."

"Going back? After everything we did to disappear? You do realize I dyed and cut my hair, don't you?"

He grinned. "Yeah, I'm surprised you went for that. It was way too easy."

She threw a French fry at him.

He ducked and laughed, but his grin quickly faded. "No one is going to see us. We'll be in and out in just a few minutes. Then we'll lie low."

"In and out of where?"

He didn't answer until they reached his car in the parking lot. "We're going to your office. I need to look at more of your files." He'd already reviewed the ones she'd gotten earlier. Buresh had come through with the subpoena, so even though Darby felt guilty letting him invade her clients' privacy, at least she could defend her actions by saying there was a court order.

"What else do you think you need from my office?"

"I want to expand the search, figure out which one of your patients is the lunatic trying to kill you."

She gritted her teeth. "They aren't patients,

they're clients. And you need to get over your prejudices. None of my clients are the type of person to go after someone with a bomb."

He gave her a droll look. "I'd bet that most of your *clients* are the kind of people who would try to blow someone up, or shoot them, or stab them. I'm betting our bomber is one of those charity cases where you got a murderer off with a light sentence because you think he's—" he held up his fingers and did air quotes "—not responsible for his actions."

Darby sucked in a breath. "Just because someone makes a mistake, it doesn't mean they're bad. It means they messed up. Someone like you should have more sympathy for the people I defend."

He stilled. "Someone like me?"

Alarm bells went off in her head, but she couldn't stop. She was so furious and sick of his condescending comments about her work. "For a man who cheated on his wife, you sure don't cut anyone else any slack for making mistakes."

His jaw tightened so hard his skin turned white beneath the stubble. "Get in."

She immediately felt contrite. She knew she'd gone too far. "Rafe, I—"

"Now."

She slid into the passenger seat and Rafe slammed the door.

AFTER AN INCREDIBLY crazy day, starting with a bombing and ending with Darby and Rafe retrieving a second backup hard drive from her office, they were spending another evening in another hotel room, sitting at a small dining table with both his laptop and hers. Rafe was taking turns searching on both computers. Darby was sitting beside him, thoroughly bored, wishing he'd talk to her.

The man was a master of the silent treatment.

He clicked another key and the pictures the bomber had sent were displayed on the screen. Darby stared at the pictures, and realized three of them had some very interesting things in common. "Zoom in on that picture on the left, the one of you."

He moused over the picture and clicked. His likeness filled the screen. Darby studied the background.

"Okay, now Jake's picture."

Rafe clicked again. Another close-up shot, but with a few more details in the background. Excitement churned through Darby. "Now my picture."

When her picture was displayed, she fist-pumped in the air.

Rafe looked at her as if she were crazy.

She grinned. "Those pictures were all taken at the courthouse, *in the same courtroom.*"

His eyes widened. He studied her picture, squinting as if he could make the background come into focus if he stared hard enough.

"Here." Darby pointed to one of the fuzzy shapes. "See that woman? That's Renee Harper. I can tell because I recognize her suit. It's her Thursday suit."

"Her...what?"

"Renee wears the same five suits every week. That's the suit she wears on Thursdays. She's Judge Thompson's—"

"Favorite court stenographer. I know that much. Can't say I've noticed her suit fetish, though."

"It's not a fetish. A fetish is usually sexual in nature. It provides a sexual release. Trust me, Renee isn't excited over her suits. She's obsessive-compulsive. You should see her in the ladies' room at the courthouse. Everything in threes. She flushes the toilet three times, pumps the soap three times, rinses her hands..."

The corner of Rafe's mouth twitched, as if he was struggling not to laugh.

Darby crossed her arms. "Put your picture back up."

"Yes, ma'am." He punched the keyboard.

She pointed to the background. "There she is. You can barely see her, but—"

"She's wearing her Thursday suit."

"Exactly. Now put my picture up again. Renee's

not in this picture, but Judge Thompson is. That's his right arm, right there on the edge of the shot."

"His arm? Let me guess. You recognize the watch, the lucky watch he wears only on Thursdays, and only when there's a solar eclipse."

She punched his arm. "Don't be silly. I know it's his arm because of his robe."

His mouth twitched again. "His robe?"

"The sleeve of his robe is snagged. Judge Thompson has a nervous habit of scratching at the fabric. All of his robes have marks on the sleeves."

He stared at her again, his brows climbing to his hairline. "Are you always this observant?"

"I hadn't really thought about it, but I suppose so."

"What do *I* do?"

"What do you mean?"

He crossed his arms. "What kind of odd habits have you noticed about me? Or am I perfect?"

"Ha! Far from it." She raised her fingers to tick off each point. "For starters, you're way too bossy. You frown too much. Your temper—"

"Forget I asked," he said, his voice dry. "I suppose you have a theory about why the pictures were all taken in the same courtroom."

"Actually, no. I don't have a theory."

"Don't sound so disappointed," Rafe said. "I think you're on to something. If we focus only on cases tried in Thompson's courtroom, that could significantly reduce the number we have to sort through."

He pulled out his phone. "I'll let Buresh know what you came up with. It might be the break we need."

Darby left him to his phone call. She crossed to her bed and sat down amidst the pile of folders and papers strewn across the comforter. She was sick of sitting at the table, going through computer files. She'd rather look at the files that were printed out.

Not the most exciting way to spend an evening in a hotel with a hot-looking guy. It was getting harder and harder to hide her growing fascination with him. Sometimes she caught him looking at her, and she wondered if he was remembering the way he'd touched her back at the hospital. But then he'd look away, his jaw would tighten, reminding her that even if he did desire her, there was no possibility of a relationship between them. He was too stubborn, too closed-minded, too set on a world of black-and-white when her world was full of gray.

"Darby, are you listening?"

She looked up, surprised to see Rafe standing beside the bed. His grim expression told her what he was going to say before he said another word.

"There's been another abduction."

DARBY WAS STILL REELING from the news that another victim had been abducted. But she and Rafe were trying not to dwell on how awful that was. Instead, they were brainstorming, trying to come up with a list of suspects.

"You said his latest victim is a private investigator?" Darby said from her perch on the foot of her bed.

Rafe looked down at her, his hands shoved into his pockets. "Yes, Clive McHenry. I've never worked with him on a court case before, so that seems to blow the theory that all the victims were related through Judge Thompson's courtroom."

"You said you've never worked with him on a *court* case. Does that mean you've worked with him in some other capacity? You knew him?"

He was quiet for so long she thought he wasn't going to answer.

"I knew him. Let's leave it at that." His voice was nearly as cold as his eyes.

"But if you knew him, and he—"

"Drop it, Darby. I'm not going to discuss it."

She waited, but he remained silent. She let out a long sigh. "Okay, we won't discuss how you knew him. But I don't want to drop the Judge Thompson angle just yet. Maybe McHenry was involved in a court case and you just don't remember."

"Or *you* don't," he said, his eyes lighting with

renewed interest. "Do you use private investigators in your casework?"

"Sometimes. We do background checks so we know the kind of person we're dealing with, and whether he's being honest with us. But the name McHenry doesn't ring any bells."

He grabbed her hand and pulled her to her feet. "Let's see if it rings any search-engine bells."

Darby laughed and sat down in front of her laptop. "All right, I'll see what I can find." She opened the directory with her files and performed a quick search. "No files with McHenry in them. Is he independent or part of a larger firm?"

"A firm." Rafe stood behind her. He gave her the name of the private investigation agency that employed McHenry.

Again, her quick search didn't get any hits. On a hunch, she broadened the time frame to include all of her archived files, regardless of date. The search took several minutes. Rafe pulled up a chair beside her and propped his chin in his palm while they waited.

A few minutes later, he straightened. "You've got a hit."

Excitement surged through Darby. She opened the file and quickly read the summary. "Looks like I hired McHenry's firm to do a background check on a client."

"Looks like? You don't remember hiring them?"

"I focus on therapy. Mindy…" She swallowed hard, and forced thoughts of her friend lying in the hospital out of her mind so she could concentrate. "Mindy took care of ordering background checks. Although this one was well before she started working for me, so a different assistant ordered this one. The client's name was Jerry Fullerton."

"That name sounds familiar."

"It should. He was a defendant in one of your cases."

"Let me guess. You testified in his defense."

"Actually, no. It looks like I testified for the prosecution. I guess that disproves your theory that I always testify on the *wrong* side."

"I didn't say you always were on the wrong side, just usually." He added a smile, as if to take away the sting of his words. "What was the date of the trial?"

"About five years ago." She rattled off the exact date.

He pulled his computer in front of him and brought up one of the police databases.

His fingers flew across the keys, typing criteria into the search engine. He punched Enter and sat back to wait. It only took a few seconds for the result to fill the screen, a detailed report from the case file.

He whistled long and low. "Fullerton did a stint in the army as an EOD specialist."

"EOD?"

"Explosive ordnance disposal, the military equivalent of a bomb technician." He read a few more lines. "This may be it. You and McHenry both worked on the prosecution side. Jake made the original arrest, and I helped him build the case. You, Jake and I all testified in that case." He read a few more lines, then looked up at her. "The judge assigned to the trial was Thompson."

"Bingo," Darby said. "What about the A.D.A., Victor Grant? Did he work the case?"

"No, doesn't look like it." He paged a few more screens in. "Wait, here he is, Victor Grant. He had a private practice back then. He was the defense attorney."

"He defended Fullerton? That doesn't make any sense, does it? If Fullerton is the bomber, and he wanted to get back at the people on his case, why would he go after his own lawyer?"

Rafe shrugged. "Maybe because his lawyer didn't get him off? Fullerton was convicted of second-degree murder." He typed a few more search strings, and another report filled the screen. "He was paroled a little over a year ago."

"He only served four years for murder?"

"First offense, crowded jails, good behavior. It happens. I'll give this information to Buresh and get the guys back at the station digging in. Fullerton's on parole, so he has to check in with his parole officer on a regular basis. We'll get his address and pick him up. Simple." He punched the information into an email and pressed Send. "You, Darby Steele, are a very smart lady." He leaned over and pressed his lips to hers.

She wasn't sure who was more surprised, Rafe or her.

He jerked back. "Sorry. I'm going to grab a quick shower. Then I'll check with Buresh, see what comes of the Fullerton lead. With any luck, this could all be over in a couple of hours."

He didn't wait for her response. He grabbed his duffel bag and headed into the bathroom. Darby reached a shaky hand up to touch her mouth. That brief touch of Rafe's lips on hers had her flushing hot all over. But to Rafe it had meant nothing, a mistake, something to apologize for.

She was glad the case was coming to a close. She desperately needed to regain control of her emotions and get off this crazy roller coaster.

The sun was going down, and the motel room plunged into darkness, but Darby didn't move. A moment later, Rafe came out of the bathroom. His hair, newly shortened at the same salon where Darby had gotten her hair cut, was slightly damp. His broad shoulders were showcased in a fresh, dark blue collared shirt tucked into a pair of casual khaki pants. The man looked good enough to eat, but she'd never be invited to that table.

"Darby?"

He was waving his hand, as if to catch her attention. She'd been staring at his chest and must have zoned out. She smiled, until she saw the cell phone clutched in his hand and the serious expression on his face. "What is it? What's happened? Did they find McHenry?"

"Not yet. Fullerton only checked in with his parole officer once, right after he got out of prison. His parole officer reported him missing, of course. Officers asked his known friends and family members if they'd seen him, but they didn't do much more than that. Lack of resources. No one knows where he is."

Chapter Fourteen

After finding out about McHenry and Fullerton, Rafe and Darby spent the night and most of the following day in the hotel waiting and hoping for good news—news that never came. Now they were driving down the highway again. Darby longed to go home, to her house on the beach, and let her stress wash away with the outgoing tide. But that day didn't seem as if it was going to come anytime soon. Not until Fullerton was in custody.

Rafe drove past another hotel, the first one they'd seen in the past twenty minutes, but he didn't stop. He was too busy on the phone with Buresh, discussing the ongoing investigation and the hunt for Fullerton. After Rafe ended his call, and passed another hotel a few minutes later, Darby started to wonder if he was ever going to stop.

"Is tonight's hotel in Miami?" she joked.

He didn't even smile. "Not quite. We're not going to a hotel. We're staying somewhere more remote, safer."

"Safer?" Her stomach clenched and she glanced at her side mirror. No other cars were on the road. No one was following them. "You've been awfully quiet since your last phone call with Buresh. Has something else happened?"

He sighed heavily and pulled the car to the side of the road. Turning in his seat, he took her hand in his. She wished he hadn't, because her pulse started slamming the moment his fingers touched hers. Then again, maybe that was good. When he touched her she had a hard time focusing on the bad things around her. And from the serious look on his face, she had a feeling she would need his touch to anchor her from whatever he was about to say.

"How much do you remember about the Fullerton case?"

"Not much. It was a long time ago. My case notes were sparse. Basically, I interviewed him several times and determined he was competent to stand trial. He knew right from wrong at the time of the murder."

"If he's the one who committed the murder."

She tensed, her hand clutching his. "What are you saying?"

"It was a circumstantial case," he said. "No blood. No fingerprints, based on eyewitness testimony placing him at the scene, some fibers and hair. Motive was supported by a recording on the victim's answering machine."

"His girlfriend. He threatened to kill her after she broke up with him. I remember," Darby said.

"There was no GSR on his hands, or his clothes."

"Gunshot residue?"

He nodded. "Fullerton was picked up a couple of hours after the shooting. He tested negative for GSR, and the murder weapon was never found."

"But...GSR washes off, right?"

"Yes. Eventually."

"I don't understand," Darby said. "The jury convicted him. Has something changed? Did a witness recant their testimony?"

"No one recanted, but eyewitnesses can make mistakes." He drew in a deep breath and checked the mirrors. "The guys at the station dug into Fullerton's alibi. He'd claimed all along he was at a minor league baseball game in Jacksonville, but no one at the ballpark remembered him. He didn't keep his ticket stub. He said he'd paid cash, so there wasn't an electronic record of anything. Buresh had the guys dig deeper. He had them look into back issues of Jacksonville's daily paper, the *Times-Union*. They found a sports feature for the ball game Fullerton said he attended. One of the pictures with the article showed some fans sitting in the stands." His hand tightened on hers. "Fullerton was one of those fans."

Darby's stomach sank. *No, he had to be wrong. If he was right, that meant...* She swallowed hard.

"He could have left the game early. That doesn't prove anything."

"The background in the picture has specific details to nail down when the picture was taken. It seems highly likely the photograph was taken a few minutes *after* Fullerton's girlfriend was murdered. The ballpark is forty-five minutes from the vic's house."

She shook her head. Part of her knew she was being irrational, but she couldn't accept what he was telling her. "Time of death isn't always exact. The coroner could have—"

"Time of death isn't in question. Neighbors heard the shot, called the police. They were on the scene within minutes."

Darby started to shake.

Rafe leaned over and pulled her against him. He rubbed his hand down her back and cradled her head against his chest. "It's not your fault. It's not anyone's fault. These things happen."

She clutched his shirt in her fist. "We sent an innocent man to prison. We destroyed his life. We—"

He eased back and put his hand beneath her chin, gently forcing her to look at him. "Stop blaming yourself. If this is anyone's fault, it's Fullerton's attorney's fault. He should have dug deeper, like we just did, to prove his client's alibi. We presented the facts as we knew them. And you..." He rubbed his thumb against her cheek in a soft caress. "All you did was testify that he was competent to stand trial—which he was. You didn't do *anything* wrong."

She nodded miserably, desperately trying to believe what he was saying.

His gaze dipped to her mouth, then, slowly, deliberately, he cupped her face in his hands and pressed his lips to hers.

She was so startled she froze, expecting him to jerk back, like the last time he'd kissed her. But instead, he deepened the kiss. She shuddered and curled her fingers against him, pulling him closer. The dark shadows of the past faded. He kissed away every thought, every hurt. Teasing, tasting, his tongue tracing erotic circles with hers.

Her belly tightened and she moaned deep in her throat. How long had it been since she'd been held like this? The answer slammed into her. Never. She'd never been held or kissed like *this*. When Rafe's lips moved against hers, heat shot through her from the top of her head to the soles of her feet. How could he make her feel cherished and treasured and make her crave him with an intensity that was frightening, all at the same time?

When he ended the kiss, the sense of loss was palpable. She didn't want him to stop. As if he knew what she was feeling, he didn't pull back right away. His lips lingered against the corner of her mouth. Then he moved to her jawline, the column of her throat. He worshipped the sensitive skin on her neck, making her shiver with longing.

She breathed his name. "Rafe."

His arms tightened around her and he buried his face against her neck. He drew a deep breath, his hard chest pressing against hers. Then he pulled back, pressed one more soft kiss against her lips and let her go.

They both sat back in their seats, staring out the windshield. Darby struggled to draw a normal breath, and from the sound of Rafe's harsh breathing, he was struggling just as much as her.

Gradually the sensual haze he'd built in her began to fade. Her breathing returned to normal. Her heart stopped pounding in her chest and slowed to a steady rhythm.

And all the earlier doubts and recriminations slammed back into her.

"We sent an innocent man to prison," she whispered.

"Yes." His voice sounded defeated, broken, telling her he was thinking about Fullerton again, too.

"We ruined his life."

Hesitation, then he murmured "Yes."

Darby turned to look out the window as Rafe pulled back onto the highway.

AT ANY OTHER TIME in Darby's life, if a devastatingly handsome man had taken her to a cozy cabin in the woods, miles from civilization, she'd have been excited. And she would have been awed by the pristine beauty surrounding her.

She would have stood by the lake behind the cabin, watching the sunset turn the water from deep blue to a rich burned gold. She would have marveled at the majestic, centuries-old oak trees, their thick branches clacking against each other in the light breeze that was picking up, carrying the scent of pine sprinkled in with the oaks.

But not today.

Because today she'd found out she'd helped destroy a man's life, and that he in turn had then destroyed other lives. Victor Grant was dead. Mindy still hadn't awoken from her coma, and probably never would. Clive McHenry was missing.

Darby's shoulders sagged. She was just about to climb the steps to the front porch when lightning zigzagged overhead, flashing against the backs of the dark clouds rolling in, snuffing out the last of the sun's light. Thunder rumbled, and the scent of rain was heavy in the air.

"It's not safe to keep standing out here." Rafe held the front door open, waiting.

His words had Darby fisting her hands and glancing around, expecting Fullerton to jump out at her from a nearby bush.

Rafe's face softened with regret. "I was referring to the lightning. Or did you forget we live in the lightning capital of the world?"

She couldn't help but smile. "I wonder if the tourists realize that when they come to visit the *Sunshine State*."

She hurried up the front steps, just making it onto the covered porch when the first fat raindrops started pinging onto the metal roof.

The tour Rafe gave her didn't take long. There wasn't much to see. A great room downstairs, with an open kitchen, and a full bath. A wrought-iron spiral staircase that led to the open loft master bedroom and bathroom.

He set her suitcase beside the dresser, having left his duffel bag downstairs. Darby didn't feel right taking the bed and making him sleep on the couch, but she knew there was no point in arguing. Rafe was old-fashioned, always opening doors, carrying her bag when she could have carried it herself. He'd probably be horrified if she suggested she sleep on the couch.

"Is it yours?" she asked, waving her hand as if to encompass the entire cabin.

He crossed his arms and leaned against the side of the dresser. "It is now. Dad's arthritis pretty much keeps him home these days. But when I was a kid, we used to come up here for a whole month every summer—fishing, shooting, canoeing. Good times."

"We?"

"My brothers, dad, me…and Trina."

"Trina is your mom?" Darby ran her hand across the forest-green comforter on the bed, smoothing out the wrinkles.

"My middle sister, Katrina. She could outfish all of us, and outshoot everyone but Lance."

"Lance…your youngest brother?"

"You remembered."

"Told you. I'm a good listener."

"So I hear."

The lack of sarcasm in his voice surprised her. A few days ago he probably would have added a snide comment about her being a therapist. Instead, he quietly watched her, a half smile on his lips. Maybe being here in this cabin where he had so many good childhood memories was a balm for his soul with everything else going on.

She envied him that, envied the closeness he obviously shared with his family, memories he treasured.

Instead of memories he wanted to forget.

"Do you want to talk about it?" His deep voice cut through the dark thoughts swirling through her mind.

"Talk about what?"

"Whatever makes you so sad when I talk about family."

She stiffened and snatched her hand back from the comforter. "I'm sure I don't know what you mean."

"Was it really that bad? Your childhood?" His mouth tilted up at the corner. "I'm a good listener."

She shot him an annoyed glance and grabbed her small suitcase from the foot of the bed. "I'm going to take a shower. And after that, I'll probably go to bed. It's been a…trying day. Good night." She hurried into the bathroom and closed the door.

RAFE CHECKED EVERY WINDOW, the front door, the sliders that opened onto the back deck. Everything was secure, but the lightning and thunder outside, along with the tinny sound of rain pounding down on the roof, made it difficult to hear any other sounds from outside besides the storm. If the killer somehow managed to figure out where Rafe had taken Darby and he drove up to the cabin right now, Rafe doubted he'd even hear the sound of the car's engine.

That made him nervous as hell, especially since he was on the first floor and Darby was on the second.

Lightning cracked overhead, followed by a boom so loud it made Rafe wince. The lights flickered, and the cabin plunged into darkness.

He yanked his gun out of his holster and held it pointing down to the ground because he didn't want to risk shooting Darby. He didn't move for several moments, listening intently for any sounds that didn't belong in the cabin. But all he heard was the storm.

And the shower running upstairs.

Having grown up in a house with three sisters, he knew what *they* would do if the lights went out while they were in the shower. First they'd scream, then they'd run out of the bathroom.

But Darby hadn't made a sound.

That uneasy feeling Rafe had felt earlier kicked into hyperdrive. Guided by his familiarity with the layout downstairs, he hurried through the dark into the kitchen. A red, blinking LED light guided him straight to the flashlight mounted on the wall charger.

He positioned the flashlight at his shoulder, holding it like an ice pick, ready to use it as a weapon if it came to that. With his gun still aimed at the floor, he clicked the flashlight on and made a quick sweep of the room. Windows and doors still secured. He turned the flashlight off and lifted the edge of the curtains from the front window. A few seconds later, the flash of lightning illuminated the porch and yard beyond.

Nothing. No other cars, no stranger skulking through the grass or hiding on the porch.

But Darby still hadn't made a sound. She hadn't called out to him in the dark. And the shower was still running.

Rafe forced his breathing to remain slow and steady as he made his way to the spiral staircase.

He turned the flashlight back on, sweeping it up the stairs to the loft. Then he hurried up the stairs to the bedroom. Empty. And there wasn't a door to the outside from this room, no balcony that would allow the killer to gain access to the bedroom without coming up the spiral staircase.

The odds of someone else being in the house besides him and Darby had just gone down close to zero, but he still wasn't taking any chances. He held his gun down to his side and stood to the right of the bathroom door.

"Darby, it's Rafe. Open the door."

Nothing, just the sound of water running.

"Darby, I'm coming in." Still nothing. Rafe tried the knob. It wasn't locked. He slowly turned it, then shoved the door open and ran inside.

He shined his light around the room. Clear. No one hiding, ready to jump out at him. The only place left was the shower.

He hurried over and yanked open the shower curtain.

Darby was curled up in the tub, her eyes wide and glassy.

Rafe cursed and set his gun and flashlight on the bathroom counter. He shut off the water and crouched by the tub.

"Darby? Can you hear me?" He smoothed her

wet, dripping hair back from her face, but she didn't even flinch at his touch. She stared into space, just like she had back at the hospital. What the hell had happened to her to make her this scared of dark, enclosed spaces?

He stood and reached for his gun. He shoved it into his holster, then grabbed the towel off the rack and tucked it in around Darby. He scooped her out of the tub and cradled her against his chest, grabbed the flashlight and carried Darby into the bedroom.

He put the flashlight on the nightstand with the light shining up at the ceiling and tried to put Darby in the chair next to the bed, but she made a tiny whimper and clung to him. The lost, terrified look in her unfocused eyes had him stiffening with rage. He suddenly wanted to find whoever had hurt her in her past and tear them limb from limb.

With Darby clinging to him, he made a quick decision. To hell with being a gentleman and preserving her modesty. She was scared and shivering. He was going to hold her and keep her warm, and try to make her feel safe. She could yell at him later for what he was about to do.

He held her with his left arm, and used his right arm to put his gun on the nightstand. He raked the covers back on the bed, sat, turned and stretched out with her beside him, facing him. He pulled the covers up over both of them. The room was still dark, but with the flashlight on, there was enough light that he could see her. He stared into her vacant eyes, waiting for her to come back to him.

He used the end of the towel to gently blot her hair. Minutes dragged by. The storm continued to boom overhead. Lightning flashed against the windows.

Even with the rain cooling everything outside, with the power out and the air conditioner off, the room began to heat up. Rafe threw the comforter off them and covered Darby's naked body with the towel.

Soon he was easing away from her, pulling his shirt up over his head. He shucked off his jeans, and would have taken off his underwear, too, except that he didn't want to shock Darby when she came out of her trance.

He wished he'd spoken to the psychiatrist at the hospital. Rafe had no idea what to do for Darby, other than hold her.

He knew the exact moment she "woke up." Her eyes widened and she drew in a shocked gasp as her gaze fell to his naked chest. Then she looked down at her towel, and Rafe could see the memory of what had happened coming back. Her hands flew up, covering her face. "I can't believe I zoned out like that again. I can't imagine what you must think of me."

He gently but firmly forced her hands back down, holding them, until she quit trying to tug them away. "What I think is that something terrible happened to you to make you scared of dark, tight places. That's not your fault, and doesn't make me think any less of you."

She drew in a shaky breath. "Thank you. And... thank you for...rescuing me from the shower." She gave him a wobbly smile.

"How much do you remember?"

Her gaze dropped from his and she chewed her bottom lip. "Everything. I always do. Later. Once I... Once I'm myself again. But...during...it's like I'm frozen, paralyzed, unable to move, or even really think."

"This has happened before, even before the hospital?"

She nodded. "And before you ask, yes, I've had therapy. Years of therapy. It's why I became a therapist myself, so I could help others the way someone once helped me."

"Looks to me like whoever 'helped' you didn't finish the job."

She tried to yank her hands back. He let her have one of them, but he kept her right hand anchored securely in his left, entwining his fingers with hers and resting their joined hands on the mattress between them.

"What happened to you?" He rubbed his thumb in slow circles back and forth across her knuckles and waited.

Finally, she swallowed, and met his gaze again. "I was seven, on summer break from school. My mom and dad took us kids to my grandma's for a visit. She lived in an old farmhouse outside of town, on farmland that wasn't farmed anymore. There were run-down chicken coops and barns, trees to climb. Paradise for five young kids. When the weekend was over, everyone else went home, but I stayed. Grandma had always favored me, the oldest grandchild. She wanted me to visit a little longer. Mom and Dad were supposed to pick me up the next day."

She shuddered and closed her eyes. Rafe released her hand and ran his fingers through her hair, feathering it back from her face.

"Go on," he urged.

"My parents didn't come back for me the next day. Or the day after that. They didn't call, either. I was getting bored. Granny didn't do a lot besides watch TV. So I went outside to play. I followed a trail into the woods, found an old shack out there, played house. I...was walking in the clearing beside the shack and I found this old, abandoned well. I was leaning over the edge, looking down, when..."

Rafe kept stroking her hair, waiting, giving her the time she needed.

"I fell," Darby continued. She squeezed her eyes shut. "It was so dark. The water was cold, ankle deep. And there were rats...and bugs...and

I screamed, and screamed, and…" She swallowed again, making a whimpering sound in her throat. "But no one came for me. No one came. No one answered my cries."

She opened her eyes, and the bleak look had Rafe's heart aching in his chest.

"I climbed out of that well all by myself. No one ever came for me. They abandoned me. It took me three days of trying to climb out, but I did it. I don't remember what happened after that. I just… I don't remember anything until months later."

"Did you ever find out what happened?"

"What do you mean?"

"Your grandmother must have been worried sick. She must have searched everywhere for you. She—"

Darby shook her head. "I never saw my grandmother again after that. I don't know what she did, or didn't do. Everyone pretended nothing had happened. My brothers and sisters gave me strange looks, tiptoed around me. Mom and Dad never spoke about it, either." She shuddered. "I left the day I turned eighteen. And I've never been back."

Rafe stroked her upper arm. Something about her story sounded familiar, as if he'd heard it before. "When did all this happen?"

The corner of her mouth quirked up and some of the sadness left her eyes. "Are you trying to find out how old I am?"

He responded to the playfulness in her tone. "Caught me."

"I'm thirty-three."

That meant her accident was about twenty-six years ago. He would have probably been in fourth grade. Had he read something, seen something on the news about what happened? Why did it sound so familiar? Maybe he'd call Buresh about it, see if he could dig something up.

"What about you?" Darby asked. "You can't ask a woman her age and not give quid pro quo."

The fear in her eyes had completely faded. Some of the pressure in Rafe's chest faded as well, and relief took its place. "Do you want that in people years, or guy years?"

"Guy years?"

"My sisters insist men mature much slower than women. According to them, I'm about twenty-six— no longer the partying frat boy, but not long enough out in the real world yet to attain real maturity. Apparently I need some gray running through my hair to be considered mature."

Darby smiled, and this time the smile made it all the way to her eyes. "I think I'd like your sisters very much. So what does that make you in people years?"

Rafe was about to respond when the lights kicked on in the bathroom, and the air conditioner turned on, sending welcome cooling air washing over his skin. He glanced toward the window, watching for lightning, listening for thunder. "Looks like the storm ended."

"I hadn't noticed."

Something in her voice made his breath catch. She was looking at him differently than she had before, reminding him of the way she'd felt in his arms when they'd shared that heated kiss in his car earlier today.

When he'd found her in the bathtub, her naked state hadn't even registered in his brain. All he'd wanted to do was get her warm and dry, and bring her back from the dark place where her mind had gone.

Now all he could think about was the nearly naked woman next to him, and that he was almost as naked as her. He needed to get out of this bed and out of this room before he did something they'd both regret.

He pulled back and reached for his jeans on the floor.

Darby's hand on his back froze him in place.

"Rafe, don't go."

Chapter Fifteen

Darby held her breath, waiting to see what Rafe would do. She wasn't normally bold, and she was shocked at herself for taking the risk that he would turn her down. If he did, she thought she might die of embarrassment.

He turned slightly, looking at her over his shoulder. "If I stay, I'm going to—"

She sat up and worked the towel off her body. She threw it on the floor and lay back on the pillows, open to his gaze. "I want you to stay...and *everything* that goes with that."

His eyes widened and dipped to her breasts. And suddenly she was in his arms. But instead of pressing his lips to hers in a fevered kiss like he'd done in the car, he grasped her shoulders and pulled her close until her breasts pressed against his chest. He looked deep into her eyes, and slowly, as if to give her a chance to stop him, lowered his mouth to hers.

Stopping him was the last thing she wanted to do. If the killer came crashing through the door right now, waving a shotgun, she still didn't think she'd stop Rafe from kissing her. She wanted this, wanted *him,* desperately.

His lips touched hers, like a match to dry tinder. She moaned and tried to get closer, sliding her hands up the contours of his chest, wrapping her hands behind his neck. He tightened his arms, crushing her against him. When he stroked her lower lip with his tongue, she opened her mouth for him, and nearly collapsed from pleasure when he worked his magic on her.

He devoured her mouth, his warm hands stroking over her skin, cupping her breasts. Her lower belly tightened, and she dropped her hands to his waist.

Darby had never been so free with her hands. She was practically a virgin, having only had sex once, and then only because she was drunk and in college, and very, very stupid. Nothing in her past had prepared her for the feelings flooding through her now.

She was hot, everywhere. Her breasts tightened almost painfully, and every little brush of Rafe's hands across her sent little zings of pleasure shooting straight to her belly.

He broke their kiss, his chest heaving as he struggled to draw a breath. "If you want me to stop, tell me now," he whispered, his voice ragged.

"Don't stop." She pressed a kiss to the base of his neck.

He groaned again and gave her another kiss before pulling back and looking into her eyes.

"It's been a long time since I've made love." He pushed her hair back from her face. "I don't know how long I can last—the first time."

She swallowed at the implied promise of more than one time. "Then I guess we'll have to keep doing this until we get it right."

He kissed the breath right out of her. Then he was filling her, stretching her, pulling her nerves taut with pleasure.

His every movement was a sensual wave of push and pull, hard and fast, driving her higher and higher on that tightrope until her nerves tightened and exploded into a dizzying wave of pleasure that had her calling out his name. Two quick thrusts and he joined her, falling with her back to the safety net beneath them.

"Morning."

Darby's eyes flew open at the sound of a deep, masculine voice next to her ear. Rafe was standing beside the bed, leaning over her, wearing a T-shirt tucked into his jeans. He pressed a kiss against her lips before she could turn away.

She pushed at his shoulders, shoving him back. "Need to brush my teeth." She covered her mouth with her hand.

Rafe laughed and moved back to lean against the

wall beside the bathroom doorway. "Fair enough. I'll just stand here and enjoy the view."

View? Darby glanced down, and let out a shriek. She was completely naked, and the sun was shining through the blinds, leaving nothing to the imagination. She grabbed the sheet from the foot of the bed and yanked it up to cover herself.

"Such a shame to cover up all that luscious skin. I especially love it when you get embarrassed. Your blush goes from your neck all the way down to your—"

"Get out of here," she said.

"I'm going to enjoy working that shyness out of you." He grinned and turned to leave.

Darby's mouth fell open when she saw the words on the back of his T-shirt—*I'm a bomb tech. If you see me running, try to keep up.* She shook her head. What was it with cops and dark humor?

She hopped from the bed and ran into the bathroom to take a shower.

BREAKFAST, OF A SORTS, was waiting for her when she came downstairs.

Rafe was sitting on a bar stool at the butcher-block countertop that separated the kitchen from the main room. A pile of cereal bars was strewn across the wooden surface. Two bottles of water sat beside the mountain of food. He waved his hand. "Whichever family member uses the cabin last is supposed to stock non-perishable food for the next person, and keep the freezer stocked. Apparently one of my sisters was the last one here because there's nothing in the freezer and we're stuck with a stash of extremely healthy and bland breakfast bars to choose from."

"What makes you think it wasn't one of your brothers who left these bars?"

He gave her a droll look. "We eat real food, not woman food."

"Woman food?"

He waved his hand at the countertop. "Low fat, low taste, high fiber."

"It's good for you." She grabbed one of the bars and peeled the foil open. "What do you normally eat for breakfast?"

"Anything I can fry in a pan."

She shook her head and took a bite of her cereal bar. Rafe seemed different this morning. Happy, less serious, more approachable. Did that mean he would answer her questions? There was so much she wanted to know about him, but one thing in particular.

She finished her cereal bar, then rested her chin in her palms while she watched him. "Why do you let Jake believe you cheated on your wife when she's the one who did the cheating?"

Rafe choked on his water. He set the bottle down and coughed several times. He turned watery eyes on her. "What makes you think she cheated on me? I thought you believed Jake's version."

"Not anymore. You've risked your life time and again for me, even when you didn't like me. There's no way you would hurt someone you loved by breaking sacred vows. Besides, it's obvious you knew who Clive McHenry was. And you admitted it had nothing to do with work. The only remaining conclusion is that it was personal. I figure you hired McHenry to see if your wife was cheating on you. So, again, why haven't you told Jake you're innocent?"

The carefree look on his face disappeared and his brows drew down. He took a long drink from his bottle of water.

Darby regretted that she'd destroyed his earlier light mood, but after last night, she knew what she wanted. She wanted Rafe. Not just for one wonderful night in a secluded cabin. She wanted more. She wanted a relationship. And to do that, she needed to understand him, to get to know him better. She didn't want a lie standing between them.

"Why haven't you told him?" she repeated.

"You don't give up, do you?" He set the bottle down on the counter, a bit more forcefully than was warranted. "Bobby Ellington—the reporter we saw at the station—he snooped just enough to figure out that McHenry had evidence about an affair. Ellington assumed I was the one cheating, and that's the story he ran in the paper."

Darby gasped. "That's terrible. Wait, are you saying you didn't dispute the story? You let it stand? That's why Jake thinks you're the bad guy?"

"The only way to make the paper run a correction would have been to prove them wrong, to show them the report...." He swallowed, his Adam's apple bobbing in his throat. "I would have had to show them the pictures to force them to print a retraction. What would be the point? Shelby was Jake's only family. He can survive losing my friendship a lot better than having his precious sister knocked off her pedestal. He would have hated me even more if I'd tarnished her memory in any way."

"You're wrong. Shelby wasn't his only family. You're his family, too. You said the two of you grew up best friends. I'll bet it's eating him up to think you hurt his sister. That's why he's so angry. Not just because he thinks you cheated, but because you two were best friends. He feels you betrayed that friendship. If you tell him the truth—"

He held up his hand to stop what she was about to say. "Spare me the therapist mumbo jumbo. I don't believe in it."

Darby fisted her hands in frustration. "What do you have against therapists? Or is it really just me?"

Rafe briefly closed his eyes. When he looked at

her again, his eyes were filled with pain. "Shelby and I saw a therapist. He was supposed to help us save our marriage. Turns out, all he did was help himself to my wife."

Darby gasped and clutched a hand to her throat. "That's why you used to despise me? Because I'm a therapist and your wife cheated on you with a therapist?"

He clamped his jaw tight, not answering.

"That's a pretty broad brush you're painting an entire profession with. Tell me, do you still feel that way? Do you think I'm a bad person, just because of my occupation?"

"I don't think you're a bad person. And I'm trying to look past your career choice."

"You're trying to…" Darby hopped off the bar stool. She was so mad she wanted to punch him. "While you're trying to look past my profession, I'll try to look past yours. After all, you'll send anyone to prison, whether they deserve it or not. You don't care if they're mentally ill, if they can't understand the consequences of what they've done."

He hopped off his seat and took a step toward her, his eyes blazing. "It's not my place to decide innocence or guilt, or even punishment. I find the facts and present them. You're the one who ignores the facts. You're the one who will do anything to get some creep off with a light sentence."

Darby crossed her arms. "All the time we've

spent together, everything we've shared, hasn't changed a thing. You still think I'm evil. And I still think you're pigheaded. Tell me, why did you sleep with me last night if you thought I was so terrible? It was just sex, wasn't it? It didn't mean anything to you."

His entire body went rigid as he stared down at her.

Some of Darby's anger faded as she watched the emotions play across his face. She was good at reading people, and she saw the hurt when she made her accusation. It was the one thing that gave her hope. She reached out toward him, ready to apologize, but he turned away.

He picked up his duffel bag from the couch. "Pack your things. We're leaving." He headed toward the door.

"Wait." Darby ran to catch up with him.

He paused at the front door.

Anger radiated off him in waves. Darby realized nothing she said right now would get through to him. She'd have to wait until he calmed down. "I thought we were going to stay here for a while. Where are we going?" she asked. "To another hotel?"

It took him several minutes to answer, as if he was trying to calm down enough not to shout. "Buresh called while you were upstairs. He wants us back at the station. He said there's a major break in the case. With any luck, you'll be back home before the day is over. And except for work, you'll never have to see me again." He yanked the door open and stepped outside.

Chapter Sixteen

Buresh met Darby and Rafe as soon as they entered the police station. He led them into a conference room where several other detectives were waiting. A folder lay on the table in front of Buresh's chair.

"Should I stay outside?" Darby asked, feeling out of place and more than a little uncomfortable with Rafe still so angry.

"Nothing that matters has changed," Rafe said. "Where I go, you go, until the killer is behind bars." He pulled out one of the chairs for her.

Nothing that matters?

She clenched her hands, ignoring the chair. "Captain Buresh, I'd prefer to wait in your office. I'm sure I'll be safe—"

"Dr. Steele," Buresh interrupted. "You both need to hear this. Please, sit down."

They all sat, and Rafe turned to Buresh. "You said there was a major break in the case."

Buresh cleared his throat, looking extremely uncomfortable. "These guys worked through the night, did some amazing detective work, the best I've ever seen. They—"

"Buresh," Rafe said, his voice impatient.

The captain folded his hands together on top of the folder. "Fullerton isn't the killer. After checking in with his parole officer that first time, he must have decided he couldn't handle the pressure again of living on the outside. Who knows? For whatever reason, he committed suicide."

Nausea roiled in Darby's stomach. She clasped a hand to her throat. Under the table, Rafe took her other hand in his. Even though he wasn't looking at her, even though she'd hurt him and he was still angry, he was trying to comfort her.

She selfishly clutched his hand like a lifeline.

"I'm sure you checked death records when you were trying to find him," Rafe said, his voice hoarse, as if Fullerton's death weighed as much on his conscience as it was weighing on Darby's. "What took so long to figure out he'd killed himself?"

"There was never a death certificate. Apparently he killed himself at his cousin's house. His *loving* cousin withdrew all of Fullerton's money from the bank. Apparently he had several thousand dollars from an inheritance. The cousin buried Fullerton in his backyard and never told anyone."

"What makes you sure the cousin didn't kill Fullerton?" Rafe asked.

"There were other witnesses. Took a while, quite a bit of pressure, but we feel we got the whole story."

Rafe nodded. "So we still don't know who the killer is."

Buresh cleared his throat again. "Actually, we do. He's Fullerton's half brother, Kurt Sonntag. Same mother, different fathers. He got sloppy when he took McHenry. It was caught on camera. And we were able to match his prints from McHenry's office with a partial from an earlier scene. He wasn't an EOD, like Fullerton, probably because the army wouldn't take him. He didn't pass the psych eval. But he's knowledgeable about explosives. As a kid, he was a fireworks fanatic who graduated to making his own explosives."

"We thought everything pointed to Fullerton earlier," Rafe said. "What makes you sure we're not making another mistake? Maybe Sonntag is another fall guy, working with the bomber, like the guy who took Mindy."

Darby's hand jerked, but Rafe's fingers tightened around hers. His thumb traced a slow circle on her wrist, as if trying to soothe her.

"Fullerton got out of prison a year ago," Rafe continued. "If Sonntag is the bomber, if he wants revenge for his brother's conviction and suicide, why wait so long?"

Darby saw the regret on Buresh's face, in the stiff lines of his body, the way he wouldn't look Rafe in the eyes. She studied the faces of the handful of detectives sitting at the table. None of them would look at Rafe.

What were they hiding?

Buresh took a deep breath. "Sonntag is a career criminal. He got out of prison a few weeks after Fullerton's suicide. He began his revenge a year ago. Then he fled to a neighboring county and got picked up for a petty crime, spent eleven months in lockup. When he got out, he came back here."

Rafe stared at him, his jaw working, as if he were trying to figure everything out. "You said he began his revenge a year ago. What did you mean?"

Buresh opened the folder in front of him and pulled out a black-and-white photograph. He set it on the table, and pushed it toward Rafe. "This is Sonntag's mug shot." He picked up another picture and set it down beside the first. "And this is a snapshot taken from the P.I.'s office. They're the same guy. Sonntag is our bomber."

Rafe stared down at the pictures without moving. His thumb stilled on Darby's wrist.

Buresh pulled a third picture from the folder. He put it over the top of the mug shot. "And this is the picture you gave me a year ago, from the security system at your house the night of the home invasion."

Darby's mouth dropped open in shock.

Sonntag, the bomber, was the man who'd killed Rafe's wife.

DARBY HAD TRIED EVERYTHING she could think of to get Rafe to talk to her. But other than one-or two-word responses, he hadn't said anything for the past hour. Instead, while the other detectives and Buresh were out trying to locate McHenry in time to save him, and had issued a BOLO for Sonntag, Rafe refused to leave the police station. He'd wanted to help find Sonntag, but since Buresh wouldn't let him, Rafe was now in Buresh's office, typing like a madman on his laptop, trying to figure out on his own where Sonntag might be.

The phone on Buresh's desk rang, startling Darby. She'd been half dozing in the chair, watching Rafe type on his computer. He picked up the phone and listened for a minute, then he warned whoever was on the phone to be extra careful on this one. He hung up and looked at Darby.

"They've spotted both Sonntag and the P.I. in an abandoned hotel scheduled for demolition, about forty-five minutes west of town. The P.I. has a bomb strapped to his chest and Sonntag is sitting next to him in a chair. Everyone's on the way there. Looks like it could be a hostage standoff."

Relief flooded through Darby. "It's over then. For us, at least. I mean, they've found him. He can't get away, right? This is good news."

He shook his head, looking unconvinced.

"It's not good news?"

"It's too easy. It doesn't feel right."

"You said they saw him. Is Buresh there?"

"Buresh is there."

"He knows what Sonntag looks like. Don't you trust him?"

Rafe tapped his hands on the desk. "I don't trust *Sonntag*. The bastard killed my wife, and he's been playing games with us. I just don't see him being stupid enough to let himself get caught like this."

"He got caught breaking and entering. He's obviously not that smart."

"I read the case file on the B and E a few minutes ago." He motioned toward his laptop. "Sonntag was tight with his brother. He was still grieving, high on alcohol and drugs when he broke into that home. That's the only reason he got caught." He shoved back from his desk. "Come on, we're leaving. If this is a decoy, some way to get the station to empty out, I don't want you caught in the middle. I'm taking you back to the cabin."

TEN MILES OUT OF TOWN, Rafe cursed and wheeled the car around in the middle of the road.

Darby grabbed the middle console and armrest to steady herself. "What's going on?"

"I've got a feeling."

"A feeling? About what?"

He floored the gas to get around a car, dodging

back into his lane when a semi honked its horn, narrowly missing them.

"What are you doing?" Darby cried out, when Rafe floored the gas again, whipping around two cars this time before yanking the wheel to avoid another car.

"He was giving us clues and we didn't even realize it. Remember those pictures? The ones of Jake, you and me? What did they all have in common?"

"The courtroom? You're going to the courthouse?"

"No, it's Sunday. The courthouse wouldn't be open. That's not where he's going."

"Where who's going?"

"Sonntag."

"He's not going anywhere. He's at a hotel west of town. Surrounded by police, remember?"

He yanked the wheel, heading down a narrow dirt road with oak trees hanging over it, blocking out most of the sunlight. "Think about it. When Sonntag took the A.D.A. to that warehouse, he tied him to a chair, strapped a bomb to him and left. When he put that bomb on Jake, he took off. He doesn't stick around to get caught or to blow himself up."

Darby nodded, agreeing with him, and starting to see where he was going with this. "So, the hotel is a decoy, somehow. They think Sonntag is there with the P.I., but he isn't."

"Right. He staged the scene to trick the cops, to get them out of town so he could go after the most important victim on his list, the one person ultimately responsible for sending his brother away. The one person in common with everyone else in those photographs."

Darby blinked. "Judge Thompson."

"Exactly. And in a town this small, everyone in law enforcement knows where Thompson can be found on a Sunday afternoon when the weather is sunny and clear and the wind isn't up."

He drove in silence for a while, racing so fast down the narrow, twisting road that Darby had to shut her eyes to keep from becoming a shaking mass of nerves.

He turned the wheel again and raced into a parking lot, passing the startled valets. He didn't stop at the clubhouse. He didn't even slow down when the car reached the green. He kept on going, right onto the pristine, manicured lawns of the Tournament Players Club golf course at Sawgrass.

DARBY BRACED HER HAND against the dashboard as the car bucked and slid on the soft grass. "What if you're wrong? What if the hotel isn't a decoy?"

Rafe glanced over at her. "Then I'm going to be in big trouble."

"How are you going to find Judge Thompson out here?"

"Just look for a man in a bright orange shirt with purple-and-yellow-striped pants."

"Are you kidding?"

"Nope. He's as predictable as Renee and her Thursday suits. Which means he should be right around the fifth or sixth hole about now."

"How do you know all this?"

He gave her a droll look. "Everyone knows about Thompson's golf habit."

"I didn't."

He shrugged.

"There!" Darby yelled, pointing up the hill. "Is that him?

An older man in a bright orange shirt was racing down the fairway in a golf cart, coming toward them. He was driving so fast people were diving out of his way. A young teenager was riding with him. And from the look on his face as he held on to the golf cart, he was terrified.

Rafe pulled the car to a stop on the path and jumped out to intercept Thompson. Darby hopped out and ran after him.

The judge slammed the brakes, making the cart slide sideways, narrowly avoiding Rafe.

Rafe put his hand out as if to steady the older man. "Are you okay, sir?"

Thompson swatted his hand away. "I'm fine, Detective Morgan. Especially now that I've found you."

Rafe exchanged a startled glance with Darby. "*You* were looking for *me*, sir?"

Thompson nodded. "I was at the fifth hole when this young man found me." He waved toward the scared-looking teenager still sitting in the golf cart, his hands wrapped around the railing on the side of his seat. His collared shirt bore the TPC logo.

"That young man gave me an envelope that a courier delivered to the clubhouse. As soon as I opened it, I knew I needed to call you." He leaned into the backseat of the golf cart and held out a large manila envelope toward Rafe.

"Just a minute, sir." Rafe pulled his ever-present pair of latex gloves out of his pocket.

He took the envelope and opened it. When he reached inside, instead of a timer, he pulled out a cell phone with a note taped to the back.

Judge Thompson leaned close to Darby. "The note says to give the cell phone to Detective Rafe Morgan immediately, that a life is at stake. Then it says something like 'an eye for an eye.' That's why I was going to the clubhouse to call him."

She nodded and watched as Rafe reached back into the envelope. Darby expected him to pull out a picture of Judge Thompson. But when Rafe pulled out the picture, his face went white. Darby rushed to his side. Her stomach sank when she saw the handsome face smiling up at her from the photograph.

Nick Morgan, Rafe's brother.

Chapter Seventeen

"Get out. You can't go with me. It's too dangerous." Rafe idled his car in front of the country club, glaring at Darby sitting in the passenger's seat. "Go inside with Judge Thompson. The club security will keep watch over both of you until the police arrive."

"What if this is a trick, to split us up?" Darby asked. "Then the bomber grabs me, and you have to choose between saving Nick or saving me. I saw that ending in *Batman*. It didn't end so well for the girl."

Rafe cursed and shoved the car into Drive. He took off, fishtailing out of the parking lot. He headed back down County Road 210, the same two-lane back road they'd taken from St. Augustine. He reached into his shirt pocket for his cell phone.

"I'll make the call," Darby said. "Focus on the road. Who do you want me to call?"

"Buresh. He's the first contact. Put him on speaker."

When Buresh was on the phone, Darby held it out between her and Rafe so they could both hear.

"Rafe, I was just about to call you. Sonntag wasn't in the hotel. It was a setup, a damn cardboard cutout like they have at movie premiers."

"What about McHenry?" Rafe asked.

"Dead long before we showed up."

"Then it was a diversion. To get all the cops out of town."

"Where are you?" Buresh asked.

"Ponte Vedra. I've got another envelope and a photograph of my brother Nick."

Buresh's gasp was audible through the phone.

"He also left a note," Rafe said. "'An eye for an eye,' which I pretty much read to mean he wants to kill my brother since he blames me for killing his. Get the guys digging fast on this. I want to know every location in Ponte Vedra that has anything to do with Sonntag's brother."

"You really think he'll lead you to Nick? This could all be a trick."

"He wanted me in Ponte Vedra, but he didn't count on me getting here so fast. I was here before the envelope arrived by courier that was supposed to get me here. I'm counting on that extra time to help me get the drop on him. Now get me an address. Fast!"

Darby ended the call for him.

"What do you think the other phone is for?" Darby asked, pointing to the one sitting in the console, the phone he'd pulled out of the envelope.

"It might be Nick's phone, or it might be a burn phone to trigger the bomb detonator. I don't know yet. Just don't touch it."

Rafe's phone rang, startling both of them. Darby looked at the screen.

"It's Buresh already." She pressed Speaker and held the phone between them.

"What have you got?" Rafe asked.

"Two possibles. Fullerton had a house off A1A, but that's pretty close to us here. I can get a guy out there in fifteen minutes."

"What's the other one?"

"A cemetery several miles off Palm Valley Road."

Rafe swore. "That's it. An eye for an eye. Give me the address."

Buresh gave him the location.

"Bring the cavalry," Rafe said. "We're going to need it."

"You got it," Buresh said. "Where's Dr. Steele?"

Rafe's jaw tightened. "Unfortunately, she's with me. And I don't have time to stash her somewhere. There are two lives on the line now, Darby's and Nick's."

"No," Darby said. "There are three. He's after you, too."

"She's right," Buresh said. "Don't go running in there like John Wayne. Sonntag wants to kill all three of you. Wait for backup."

"I can't wait, knowing he's got my brother." Rafe nodded at Darby to end the call. He spotted the road he was looking for and slowed the car to make the turn.

The phone rang just as he started down the gravel road. Not his phone.

The phone that was sitting in the console.

"What do I do?" Darby asked.

The phone rang again.

Rafe's eyes widened and he slammed the brakes, skidding to a halt. "Come on," he yelled. "Get out. Now, now, now." He unclicked his seat belt and unclicked Darby's. He grabbed her in his arms and hauled her with him out the driver's side.

He set her on her feet and pulled her with him toward the trees. "Run, Darby! Run!"

The car exploded behind them, catapulting them both into the air.

"STUPID, STUPID, STUPID," Rafe groaned. He held his hand to his head, wincing. He'd assumed the bomber wanted to fool him, get him to use the phone from the envelope, maybe to search through called numbers, looking for clues. He should have realized from the beginning the phone was the detonator. The bomber probably rigged a bomb under his car when he took Darby to the station.

He forced himself into a sitting position and turned toward Darby.

She wasn't there.

The fog in his brain lifted and panic slammed into him. "Darby, where are you?"

But he already knew the answer.

Sonntag had her.

RATS SQUEAKED NEXT to Darby. She swatted at one of the furry bodies, and it fell with a sharp cry into the water. A roach fell onto her face and she screamed.

"Hey, darlin'. Wake up. It's bad, I know, but I'd rather share the nightmare with you than see you suffer by yourself."

Darby opened her eyes. Nick was staring down at her, his brow furrowed with concern. What was Nick doing down in the well with her? She blinked. She wasn't in a well.

She was somewhere much, much worse.

She sat up. Nick sat next to her, his back braced against a marble wall.

"We're in a...a—"

"Mausoleum," he said. "Or crypt, if you prefer. Kind of a smelly old one at that, but not for long." He gestured toward the corner a few feet away.

Three steel pipes sat on the concrete floor with wires running out of them, and a timer sitting on top. Darby's breath caught in her throat. "I don't suppose you DEA guys know how to disable a bomb?"

"Nope, afraid I missed that class. I don't suppose you've taken a first aid class?"

"First aid? Why—"

Nick held his shirt open.

Darby's hands flew to her throat. The shaft of a knife stuck out from Nick's abdomen. Blood trickled down from the wound. "Oh, my gosh, Nick. Oh, my gosh."

He laughed, then winced. "Not exactly the words I used when it happened."

Darby bent down on her hands and knees, studying his wound. "It's not bleeding much. I don't think we should pull the knife out, though."

"Hurts like hell. I don't suppose you brought the bomb squad with you, before you were caught?"

"No, but I did bring your brother. Or rather, he brought me. Our car exploded."

Nick turned pale.

"No, no, Rafe wasn't in the car. He pulled me out. We both got out. But I don't know where he is now." She shoved to her feet and rushed to the bomb to look at the timer.

They had less than fifteen minutes.

"I'm sure he got away, and he's bringing help," Nick said.

"Right, I'm sure he is."

Darby exchanged a glance with Nick, and realized they were both lying to each other.

THE TRAIL THROUGH the woods was easy for Rafe to follow. Sonntag hadn't bothered to try to hide his footprints.

He wanted Rafe to find him.

Which meant Rafe was walking into a trap. But he didn't have a choice. He had to find Darby and Nick.

He didn't know how long he'd been in a blast-induced stupor. How much of a head start did Sonntag have? A minute? Five? More? Rafe clenched his hand around his pistol.

Hold on, Darby. Hold on, Nick. I'm coming for you. Hold on.

"IT'S A PIPE BOMB," Nick offered, his voice weak, barely above a whisper now.

Darby rolled her eyes. "Even I can figure that much out." She crouched over the ominous-looking bundle of pipes and wires, looking for…what? A sign that said Pull Here To Disable Bomb?

"Darby."

"Leave me alone, Nick. I'm thinking."

"Darby."

The urgent, low-pitched tone had her jerking around. Rafe stood at the doorway, separated from her by three feet and a very strong set of iron bars.

A sob escaped her as she ran to him. "Rafe, thank God you're okay. We're trapped. And there's a bomb. I don't know what to do. I don't—"

"Are you hurt?" He reached a hand through the bars and grasped her hand in his.

"What? No, no, I'm fine. I guess the haircut wasn't as much a disguise as we'd hoped, though, huh?" She tried for a smile but failed miserably.

He looked past her, and his jaw tightened. "Nick."

Darby heard the pain in his voice. She turned. Nick's eyes were closed. She turned back to Rafe. "He's alive. See his chest rising? But he's been stabbed. We need to get him to a hospital."

Rafe looked over his shoulder. He shoved his gun in his holster and grasped the bars. He strained and pulled, the cords standing out in his neck. He gave up, panting. "It's no use. Buresh is on the way, with the bomb squad. They'll have bolt cutters. We'll get you out of here."

"We don't have much time. The bomb…maybe you can tell me what to do. Do I just pull the wires out?"

He grabbed her hand when she started to turn away. "Don't touch it. One spark and it's over. See the timer?"

"Yes."

"How much time is left?" He half turned, watching the woods behind him.

Darby looked at the timer, careful not to touch

it. Her heart plummeted and she ran back to Rafe. "Seven minutes, give or take. What do we do?"

His gaze darted back and forth, searching out every corner of the mausoleum. Then his gaze met hers. "There may be a way. But you'll have to be strong. And you'll have to work fast."

"Anything. What?"

He reached into his pocket and pulled out a pocketknife. He plopped it in her hand.

"Do you want me to cut a wire?"

"No. There's nothing you can do to stop the bomb."

She grabbed the bars in her hands, pulling at them in frustration. "For a bomb tech, you don't seem to be very good at disabling bombs."

His mouth quirked up in a smile. "I promise I'm a lot better with a bomb suit and appropriate tools." His smile faded. He looked at her with what could only be called pity as he reached out and cupped her face with one hand and pointed behind her with the other. "You're going to have to remove one of those marble squares on that far wall. There's a screwdriver on one end of that knife. Use that."

"Marble squares?" She looked where he was pointing. Her throat tightened and she could barely breathe. "But…that's where they put the *coffins*."

"It's your only chance. You're strong. You can do this. You have to open up one of those squares and crawl inside."

DARBY'S FACE WENT PALE and she started shaking. "No, I can't... I can't."

"You have to. Pick one without a name on the front. That means it's empty. It won't be sealed. Just four little screws, one on each corner. Then use the knife to cut the caulking around the square. It should pop right off. Crawl inside. I don't know if it will totally shield you from the blast, but it's the only chance you have. Hurry, Darby. It's the only way."

The fear and panic in her eyes was killing him.

"What about Nick?" she asked. "I can't just leave him here."

Grief nearly buckled his knees. He looked at his brother, so still and quiet, lying on the floor. "There's nothing you can do for him now."

"But...I can't. Don't you see? I can't go in there. And I can't leave him. I can't abandon him."

He grabbed both her hands and pulled her close against the bars. "Look at me." He gave her a small shake. "Look. At. Me."

Her chest was rising and falling too fast. She was close to hyperventilating. He squeezed her hands and gently shook them again until she met his gaze.

"You *are* going to take off one of those marble squares, Darby. You *are* going to crawl into that dark, tight hole. And do you know why you're going to do that?"

Her lower lip trembled. "No, why?"

"Because you won't be alone. I won't abandon you. You're going to survive. And after…after the explosion, I'll be here for you. I won't abandon you. I'll search for you. And I'll find you."

She blinked several times. "You don't understand. You don't know… It's not that I won't. It's that I *can't*." Her voice broke on the last word.

How much longer did she have? Four minutes? Three? He had to get her in one of those holes in the wall, or she would die. How could he make her do something that terrified her more than the idea of a bomb exploding and ripping her to pieces?

His gaze shot to Nick. Darby was softhearted. She wanted to save everyone, and above all, she never wanted to abandon someone in need, whether they deserved it or not. He'd thought that was a flaw. Now he knew better. It was her strength. And he'd use that strength to save her life. She wouldn't go in that dark, tight hole to save herself.

But she would do it to save someone else.

"You're right," he said, purposely making his voice hard. "You can't leave Nick to die. But I can't save him. You have to save him."

Her eyes widened. "But, how—"

"Get the marble square off. Slap Nick. Punch him. Do whatever it takes to wake his lazy ass. Then make him crawl into the hole behind you." He didn't think she'd be able to wake Nick. And even if she did, Nick would probably be too weak to move. But at least with the marble square off, her preservation instincts might kick in and she'd dive into the hole before the timer ran out. "Check the timer. How much more time do we have?"

She ran to the bomb. "Three minutes!"

"Save my brother, Darby. Please. You're the only chance he's got. Go!"

She ran to the far side of the mausoleum and got down on her knees in front of one of the squares on the bottom row.

Rafe watched her unscrew one of the corners. "Good, faster, babe. Hurry. Three more."

She nodded, her movements jerky as she worked on the second corner. Then the other two corners. She reached out and tried to pry the marble square off the wall. "It won't move."

"Cut the caulking. Run the blade around the edge. Then kick it if you have to."

She did as he said, and the square fell onto the concrete floor, cracking in two.

The hairs stood up on the back of Rafe's neck. A whisper of sound had him jerking around. He dove to the ground just as Sonntag brought a tire iron down where he'd been standing moments before. The tire iron banged against the bars and fell to the ground.

Darby screamed from inside the mausoleum.

"Get in the hole, Darby! Now!" Rafe yelled. He

grabbed for his gun, but Sonntag slammed into him. The gun went flying into the trees.

SAVE MY BROTHER.

Darby didn't know if she could, but she had to try. Rafe had saved her too many times to count. And he was fighting for his life right now—and hers.

She had to try.

She ran to Nick. "Forgive me," she whispered. She bit her bottom lip, and slapped Nick hard across the face.

RAFE CIRCLED SONNTAG, desperately looking for an opening. *Damn it.* He didn't have time for this.

Darby and Nick didn't have time for this.

The welcome sound of sirens screamed up the road toward them.

Sonntag waved his knife, laughing. "They won't get here in time. Your brother will die, if he isn't dead already. And so will the girl." His lip curled in a sneer. "You're going to find out what it's like to lose everything that matters to you."

Like hell he would.

Rafe lunged at him. Sonntag dove out of the way and whirled around, hacking with the deadly blade. Rafe dodged him, but not fast enough. The blade sliced his arm, like an electric shock shooting across his bicep.

"Don't worry," Sonntag said as he stood above him. "I won't kill you yet. An eye for an eye." He pulled a phone out of his pocket.

And then Rafe knew. The timer on the bomb was fake. Sonntag wanted to control when the bomb blew, down to the second, to make Rafe suffer. He was going to use the phone to blow the bomb.

Rafe aimed a vicious kick at the other man's knee. A loud crack was followed by a howling scream as Sonntag fell to the ground, holding his leg. The phone and knife went skittering across the grass in different directions.

Rafe rolled and came up with the knife, but Sonntag grabbed his foot. Rafe twisted around, slashing down with the blade, stabbing the other man's arm.

Sonntag's roar of pain echoed through the trees but he didn't let go. He wrapped both his hands around Rafe's leg and yanked him back. Rafe lost his grip on the knife and fell to the side.

The sirens stopped. Car doors slammed. Voices echoed from the trees.

"Over here!" Rafe yelled.

Sonntag tugged the knife out of his arm. He shimmied away from Rafe, army-crawling across the grass.

Rafe's right arm hung useless, blood dripping down his fingers. He spotted Sonntag's goal, the phone, a few feet away.

"No!" Rafe lunged at Sonntag just as he turned with the knife in one hand, and the phone in the other.

Rafe ignored the knife, reaching for the phone. Burning, tearing pain sucked the air out of his lungs. He landed with a jarring thud. His teeth cracked together. Sonntag's skull slammed against the hard ground.

"Here they are," someone shouted. Another man cursed. "Medic!"

Rafe dragged himself into a sitting position. He clutched the phone in his hand, cradling it against his chest with his good arm. Beside him, Sonntag lay unmoving, staring up at the sky, a tiny line of blood running out of his ear and down his cheek. Rafe didn't know if the man was alive or dead, and he didn't care.

All he cared about was reaching Darby and Nick.

Buresh was suddenly standing over him. "Don't move. You're leaking all over the place."

An EMT knelt beside Rafe and reached for the phone. "I'll take that, sir."

Rafe twisted away. "Don't touch it." He motioned for one of the bomb techs. "Here." He handed the phone to him. "Be extremely careful with that. It's the remote detonator to the IED inside the mausoleum."

"You got it. We'll get the robot."

"Help me up, Buresh. Darby's inside with the

bomb, and Nick. He's hurt. We need to get the gate open."

Buresh hauled him to his feet. The burning pain in Rafe's chest and arm had him gasping for breath.

"I don't suppose I can convince you to wait in the ambulance." Buresh gestured toward the emergency vehicles lined up on the grass several hundred yards away.

"Not a chance." He and Buresh followed the bomb squad to the mausoleum. A quick snip with some bolt cutters and the lock gave way.

Rafe rushed inside first, shoving past the others.

Buresh followed behind him, then stopped suddenly, looking around. "I thought Nick and Darby were in here."

A ragged line of blood zigzagged across the concrete floor to an opening in the mausoleum wall. "I didn't think she'd really do it," Rafe said. "I didn't think she *could* do it. I didn't…" He rushed forward, ignoring the burning pain across his ribs. He squatted in front of the square.

"What are you talking about?" Buresh knelt beside him.

Rafe braced himself for what he was about to see. Darby was probably comatose by now, being shoved up in that dark hole. And Nick… Rafe didn't even want to admit to himself what he knew deep inside. There was so much blood.

"Give me some light in here," he rasped, trying to see inside the hole.

Buresh waved at one of the bomb techs who was examining the pipe bomb. The tech unclipped a flashlight from his utility belt and handed it to Buresh.

He clicked it on, pointing it into the hole.

Rafe peered inside. In the cold, dark tomb, two very green eyes blinked back at him. Darby raised her hand to shield her eyes, bumping her elbow in the tight space as she jackknifed around to look at him.

"Hurry, Rafe," she ordered. "The knife moved when I pulled Nick in here. I can't stop the bleeding."

He swallowed against the lump rising in his throat. "You crawled in a dark hole. You pulled Nick inside?"

She grinned. "I did! He helped a little. I slapped him like you told me to."

He would have laughed, but his heart was pounding so hard at the thought of how close she'd come to being killed that he couldn't speak.

"The bomb didn't explode," Darby said. "We didn't turn into pink clouds."

Rafe shuddered. He yelled at his fellow bomb techs. "Load and go. We've got wounded here. Let's get them out. Now!"

Chapter Eighteen

Darby wiped her palms on her slacks. She stared at the hospital room door and tried to work up the nerve to knock. She hadn't seen Rafe or Nick since yesterday, when they'd been taken away in the ambulance. After everything that had happened, why was she so afraid to open the door to their room?

She knew why. Because with the bomber dead, she had no excuses anymore to be with Rafe. Once she thanked him and said goodbye, she would go back to her life. He would go back to his. Instead of lovers, they'd be adversaries again.

No, that wasn't true. She'd never think of him as her adversary again. Because she was pathetically, hopelessly in love with him. That realization had slammed into her when she watched him being carted off in the ambulance. The sight of all that blood had nearly driven her to her knees, because it was Rafe's blood. But what good was it to realize you were in love with someone, when they weren't in love with you?

"Miss, do you need something?" A nurse paused in the hallway, a curious smile on her face.

"No, I'm… I was going to say hello to Detective Morgan, but I think maybe he's sleeping. I'll come back later."

"Have you knocked?"

"No. Wait, don't—"

The nurse rapped on the door.

"Come in," Rafe's deep voice called out from inside.

"He's awake," the nurse said, holding the door open. "Go on in."

Panic rooted Darby in place. "I've changed my mind. I—"

"I can hear you, Darby," Rafe said in a loud voice. "Get in here."

Darby wanted to kick the nurse. She forced a smile instead. "Thank you."

"Have a nice visit." The nurse headed back down the hall.

"Darby?" Rafe repeated, sounding annoyed.

Darby drew a deep, bracing breath, and entered the room.

"It's about time you came to see me," Rafe said from his hospital bed.

Darby stepped to his side. She glanced at Nick, lying in the other bed in their shared room.

"Don't worry about him," Rafe said. "He's asleep."

"No, I'm not." Nick winced and opened his eyes.

"I wish I were. You'd think the nurses were paying for the morphine out of their own pockets, as stingy as they are with it. I'm in pain here."

"Suck it up and shut up," Rafe growled. "Darby, come closer."

She bristled at his order. "You're still too bossy."

"And you're still too stubborn." His expression softened. "So stubborn you pushed through your fears and did the impossible. You saved my brother. Thank you."

Her face heated and she glanced at Nick. He propped his arms behind his head and didn't bother to pretend he wasn't watching their exchange with interest.

"I didn't save him. The bomb didn't explode."

"You still get credit. Tell her thank-you, Nick."

"Thank you, darlin', from the bottom of my heart." He rubbed his chin. "Although, if there's ever a next time, I'd appreciate it if you wouldn't hit me quite so hard to get my attention. I think you cracked my jaw." He winked as if to let her know he was teasing.

Darby nodded, feeling uncomfortable with the praise. "I'm just glad you're both going to be okay. I heard you were both extremely lucky."

"You do realize I was stabbed, right?" Nick asked in a grumbling tone.

"So was Rafe. In his arm and his chest."

Nick snorted. "He had a scratch across his ribs,

hardly a stab wound. He might have gotten more stitches than me, but I'm the one who had a knife in the gut." He grinned. "I know what will make me feel better, though. Come here, Darby."

She started to cross to him but Rafe grabbed her hand. "I don't think so."

Darby glanced between the two brothers, wondering what she'd missed. Rafe glared at Nick. Nick looked as though he was about to burst into laughter.

"Well, I…ah, wanted to thank you," she told Rafe.

He raised a brow. "Thank me?"

Why was he making this so hard? "Yes, thank you. You saved me, again. You've risked your life countless times for me now. I'll never be able to repay you for that."

His jaw tightened. "I don't want your gratitude."

"You don't?"

"No, I don't. I want—"

A knock sounded on the door. It opened to reveal a petite woman, the same woman Darby had seen in the pictures on Nick's bookshelf. Rafe and Nick's mother.

The woman let out an excited shriek. "They're both in here. Come on." She waved her hand and the room seemed to fill all at once with people talking and laughing and crying.

More people poured into the room, and Darby

found herself pushed back to the corner by the door. She waited through the tears and hugs, trying to catch a glimpse of Rafe again, but there were too many people. And as usual, everyone around her was taller than she was.

Maybe it was better this way. No prolonged goodbye. No awkward conversation.

She pulled the door open and stepped into the hall. Her feet dragged, even though she should have been relieved to leave. This hospital held no good memories for her. Rafe didn't need her. And Mindy... Darby swallowed against the tightness in her throat. Poor Mindy had a long, hard recovery ahead of her and had been moved to a rehab facility. There was no reason for Darby to want to stay.

She moved toward the elevators at the end of the hall. But when she passed one of the waiting rooms, a familiar voice had her pausing at the doorway.

Jake.

He was wearing his hospital gown because he was still a patient. Was he sitting in the waiting room, working up his nerve to see Rafe? Darby stiffened when she realized who was sitting beside Jake—the reporter Robert Ellington. The same reporter whose sloppy reporting had poisoned the relationship between Jake and Rafe.

Darby marched into the waiting room.

Five minutes later, she stepped out the door, feeling very satisfied with how things had turned out. She stopped at the elevator. When the doors opened, Captain Buresh was standing there.

He smiled and shook her hand. "Dr. Steele. Going home already?"

Home. A week ago that would have sounded good. Today it just sounded…lonely. "I guess I am. Thank you for everything."

"Wait a minute. I have something for you. I was hoping to catch you." He dug into his jacket pocket and pulled out a sheaf of papers.

"What is this?" Darby asked.

"Rafe called when you two were at his cabin. He asked if I could have one of the guys look up something for him. With everything going on, I forgot about it, but he called me this morning before the sun came up and asked me whether I had the information yet. So here I am." He handed the papers to her. "You take care, Dr. Steele." He saluted her and headed down the hall, toward Nick and Rafe's hospital room.

More than anything Darby wanted to follow him, to see Rafe one more time. Instead, she shoved the papers into her purse and stepped into the elevator.

Once she was in her car, she took the papers out, curious what Rafe had thought was so important that he'd called Buresh about it this morning.

She unfolded the stack, and immediately stilled. The first page was a photocopy of an old newspaper story. The headline read Local Girl Found in

Well After Exhaustive Search. And underneath it was a picture of her, twenty-six years ago.

Search? She didn't remember anyone searching for her. And they hadn't found her. She'd clawed her own way out.

Hadn't she?

She scanned the story, and the next one, and the next one, and by the time she was done, tears were flowing down her face so hard she couldn't see to read anymore.

"WHY DIDN'T YOU EVER tell me the truth, Mom?" Darby squeezed her mother's hand on the bench beside her. The front porch of her parents' modest home was finally empty except for the two of them. The rest of her family—her father, her brothers and sisters, their wives, husbands, children—had all rushed over in an impromptu family reunion when they found out the prodigal daughter had returned.

Not one of them had judged her, or berated her for having ignored them for over a decade.

Her mother gave her a watery smile. "It took years of therapy just to get you to talk again after falling into that well. The doctors said not to push, not to try to get you to tell us anything, that you'd tell us in your own time, on your own terms."

Darby shook her head. "All these years, I thought no one looked for me. I made up my own story, that I'd climbed out of the well on my own. That no one came for me." She looked at the little white lines on her fingers.

Her mother smoothed the lines. "You tried to climb out but you couldn't. Your daddy is the one who found you. You'd wandered off miles into the woods."

"It must have all been a dream, terrible and wonderful at the same time. I dreamed I was with Grandma, and I wandered off. But Grandma—"

"Died a year before you fell down that well."

Darby stared out at the cars lined up and down the street. She was surrounded by love. She'd always been loved and had never realized it. She'd been blind to what she had, and had never known what she'd lost.

Until now.

Darby wasn't wealthy, but she had plenty of money. Her parents had far less than her, yet they were far happier than she'd ever been. The misery Darby remembered wasn't misery because of how little they had. It was their misery that their daughter couldn't be happy, that she had withdrawn from her own family and had built a fake world to retreat into so she could cope.

"I love you, Mom."

"I know."

The front yard began to fill with her family. One by one they drifted from the backyard, giving her tentative smiles, standing in groups or watching the children play.

Darby's oldest brother leaned down and kissed his wife.

Darby's heart squeezed in her chest.

"Honey," her mother said, "you have to stop blaming yourself. Everything turned out fine. You're here now. Today is a happy day."

"I know I should be grateful. And I am, but so much has happened, so much you don't know about." She gave her mother a fierce hug, then pulled back. "Did you hear about that warehouse explosion over a week ago?"

"Where the assistant district attorney was killed?"

Darby swallowed hard. "Yes. That was an awful day. And I was there." She began to tell the story, starting with the moment Rafe Morgan had burst into her office. As she spoke, her family gathered closer, listening with rapt attention. Halfway through, her mom gave her an odd look and went inside the house.

"Go on," Darby's father urged her. "What happened next?"

By the time Darby finished telling everything, her mother was back on the porch, and there wasn't a dry eye in her entire family, except for Darby. She'd cried so much she didn't think she had a drop of moisture left for even one more tear.

Her father pulled her into a tight hug. "You're lucky to be alive, young lady."

Darby hugged him back. "I know. Rafe saved me."

Her mother shoved in between them and cupped Darby's face in her hands. "Answer me one question. Are you in love with Detective Rafe Morgan?"

Darby's face heated and she glanced at her family gathered around her.

"Mom, I can't—"

"Do you love him? One simple question, young lady. I could hear it in your voice the entire time you were telling your story. The answer is obvious to me and everyone else, but you need to admit it to yourself."

"It doesn't matter how I feel. He doesn't love me."

"Darby."

"Yes, yes, okay? Yes, I'm in love with a man who doesn't love me."

Her mother grinned and stepped to the side. "Everyone, move out of the way." Her mother waved them back.

"Mom, what are you…" Darby gasped and her hand flew to her throat.

Rafe stood at the bottom of the steps, his right arm in a sling, staring up at her. Now she knew why her mom had gone inside. She'd meddled, had called Rafe. Darby didn't know what her mom had said to him to get him to come here, and she was too afraid to hope.

"Rafe," she choked out. "What are you doing here? You should be in the hospital."

"I'm still a cop, Darby Steele."

Her hopes plummeted. "And I'm still a therapist."

He climbed the first step. "I'm still going to put as many criminals as I can behind bars."

Darby stiffened. "And I'm still going to fight you every chance I get. Nothing has changed."

Rafe climbed another step. "*Everything* has changed. Before I knew you…before I *really* knew you, I didn't understand. I never considered people's pasts, what they'd been through, what they'd suffered. I never considered that criminals might be victims, too." He raised a hand as if to stop any crazy thoughts she might be having. "I still think most of those criminals should do hard time. But now I'm willing to *consider* both sides."

He climbed another step.

Darby stood and crossed to the top step, but even with him a step below her, she had to crane her neck up to look him in the eyes. "You didn't answer my question. Why are you here?"

"I would have chosen you."

"What?"

"Remember what you said in my car, about Batman having to choose between saving two different people? It doesn't matter who the other person is.

If I had to choose, to save someone else or to save you, I would always choose you."

"Oh, that's so sweet," one of Darby's sisters whispered next to her.

Darby elbowed her in the ribs. "You still haven't answered my question. Why are you here?"

He lifted his hand to cup her face. "You left the hospital in the middle of our conversation."

She looked around at her family, her face flushing even hotter. Every one of them was staring at her. "Fine," she said. "What else did you have to say?"

"You're not going to make this easy, are you?"

"Make what easy?"

"This, I needed to tell you this." He pulled her against him and gave her a blistering hot kiss, right on the porch steps, in front of her mom, her dad, her entire family.

Darby was blinking in shock when he ended the kiss.

"I love you, Darby Steele," he said. "I want to marry you, but we haven't known each other that long. I understand if you want to date first, and take your time. But you're going to have to agree to live in sin with me. Because I can't stand the thought of not being with you. I'm not a saint. And you're way too sexy, especially when you make those little moans deep in your throat—"

She clapped her hand over his mouth.

Rafe's eyes danced with mischief, and Darby's family broke into laughter around them.

Everyone except her father.

He cleared his throat and stepped next to her. "Young lady, I'll not tolerate this kind of behavior. If you and this man have done something you shouldn't, well, then, you're going to have to make it right. Looks like you're going to have to get married." He winked and broke into a smile.

Darby looked around, overwhelmed by the love surrounding her. The tears she'd thought had long ago dried started running down her cheeks. She reached up and wrapped her arms around Rafe's neck. "I love you. You gave me back my family."

"You gave me back my best friend."

"Jake went to see you?"

"You know he did."

She shrugged, trying to appear nonchalant. "I'd hoped. I didn't know, but I'd hoped."

He brushed back her hair from her face. "You gave me something else, Darby. Something far more precious than anything I gave you."

"What's that?"

"You gave me your heart."

* * * * *

LARGER-PRINT BOOKS!
GET 2 FREE LARGER-PRINT NOVELS PLUS
2 FREE GIFTS!

HARLEQUIN®

INTRIGUE®

BREATHTAKING ROMANTIC SUSPENSE

YES! Please send me 2 FREE LARGER-PRINT Harlequin Intrigue® novels and my 2 FREE gifts (gifts are worth about $10). After receiving them, if I don't wish to receive any more books, I can return the shipping statement marked "cancel." If I don't cancel, I will receive 6 brand-new novels every month and be billed just $5.49 per book in the U.S. or $5.99 per book in Canada. That's a saving of at least 13% off the cover price! It's quite a bargain! Shipping and handling is just 50¢ per book in the U.S. and 75¢ per book in Canada.* I understand that accepting the 2 free books and gifts places me under no obligation to buy anything. I can always return a shipment and cancel at any time. Even if I never buy another book, the two free books and gifts are mine to keep forever.

199/399 HDN F42Y

Name	(PLEASE PRINT)
Address	Apt. #
City	State/Prov. Zip/Postal Code

Signature (if under 18, a parent or guardian must sign)

Mail to the Harlequin® Reader Service:
IN U.S.A.: P.O. Box 1867, Buffalo, NY 14240-1867
IN CANADA: P.O. Box 609, Fort Erie, Ontario L2A 5X3

**Are you a subscriber to Harlequin Intrigue books
and want to receive the larger-print edition?
Call 1-800-873-8635 today or visit www.ReaderService.com.**

* Terms and prices subject to change without notice. Prices do not include applicable taxes. Sales tax applicable in N.Y. Canadian residents will be charged applicable taxes. Offer not valid in Quebec. This offer is limited to one order per household. Not valid for current subscribers to Harlequin Intrigue Larger-Print books. All orders subject to credit approval. Credit or debit balances in a customer's account(s) may be offset by any other outstanding balance owed by or to the customer. Please allow 4 to 6 weeks for delivery. Offer available while quantities last.

Your Privacy—The Harlequin® Reader Service is committed to protecting your privacy. Our Privacy Policy is available online at www.ReaderService.com or upon request from the Harlequin Reader Service.

We make a portion of our mailing list available to reputable third parties that offer products we believe may interest you. If you prefer that we not exchange your name with third parties, or if you wish to clarify or modify your communication preferences, please visit us at www.ReaderService.com/consumerchoice or write to us at Harlequin Reader Service Preference Service, P.O. Box 9062, Buffalo, NY 14269. Include your complete name and address.

HILP13R

ReaderService.com

Manage your account online!

- Review your order history
- Manage your payments
- Update your address

*We've designed
the Harlequin® Reader Service
website just for you.*

Enjoy all the features!

- Reader excerpts from any series
- Respond to mailings and special monthly offers
- Discover new series available to you
- Browse the Bonus Bucks catalog
- Share your feedback

Visit us at:

ReaderService.com

RS13